SAVING THE WHALES

A Bwana Doc Adventure

By D. R. Schneider

BWANA DOC

Bwana Doc Adventures

Bwanadoc.com

Bwana Doc Adventures
P.O. Box 958
Round Rock, TX. 78680

Copyright © 2008 by D. R. Schneider
Cover Art by Amanda Nelson

www. bwanadoc.com

Vodka Monopolowa is a trademark of Altvater Gessler-J.A. Baczewski Gmbh. Hendrick's Gin is a trademark of William Grant and Sons, Ltd. Whac-a-mole is a trademark of Bob's Space Racers, Inc. Bwana Doc and the Bwana Doc skull over earth symbol are trademarks of Bwana Doc Adventures.
Printed in the U.S.A.

Publisher's Cataloging-in-Publication
(Provided by Quality Books, Inc.)

Schneider, D. R. (Dennis R.)
    Saving the whales : a Bwana Doc adventure / by D.R.
Schneider—Softcover 1st edition
        p. cm.
        LCCN 2008905459
        ISBN-13: 978-0-9820776-0-3
        ISBN-10: 0-9820776-0-2

    1. Environmentalists--Fiction. 2. Whaling--Japan--Fiction. 3. Whaling--History--Fiction. 4. Whales--Fiction. 5. Adventure stories, American. I. Title.

PS3619.C4468S28 2008   813'.6
                        QBI08-600181

Acknowledgments

To Jason Roberts for information on the types of Scotch served at the Dockside Restaurant and Bar in Wellington, New Zealand. Captain Corinna Ford with the 552nd Air Control Wing for invaluable insights into the E-3 Sentry AWACS system—an excellent example of what makes America's military second to none in defending freedom. And last, but certainly not least, my wife Zeta for her valuable comments, editing and encouragement—without her, this book would not have been written. Any errors in this book are, of course, my own.

Chapter One

Whale Killing

"If we can imagine a horse having two or three explosive spears stuck in its stomach and being made to pull a butcher's truck through the streets of London while it pours blood into the gutter, we shall have an idea of the method of killing. The gunners themselves admit that if whales could scream, the industry would stop for nobody would be able to stand it."--Dr. Harry Lillie. He worked as a ship's physician on an Antarctic whaler in the 1940s.

The ship is old. So old, that in any other fleet, she would have been sent to the scrap yard long ago. Ships that are made to kill, though, have a life of their own; perhaps they feed on their victims and that gives them a special longevity against the sea. A romantic might say that; but in reality, it was all about profit and the cost of building a specialized ship made to harvest animals that long ago were much more abundant and more in demand than they were today. Displacing over 7,000 tons, she leaves her homeport of Shimonoseki in southern Japan. She steams ahead, plowing through the light swell on her long journey to the frigid Southern Ocean that surrounds the continent of Antarctica. Her rusty sides do not stain the water anymore than they are made blue by the water that washes over them as she churns out of the harbor. She ignores the news helicopters filming her exit. She sails with her companion vessels; the catcher ships. Her name is the *Yoshino Maru* and she is a whaler factory ship, the last of her kind in the world. Her work is killing whales.

D. R. Schneider

What is a factory ship? It takes the whale caught by smaller boats called catcher trawlers, hoists it on board and its crew cuts the whale up into the parts that will be sold back in port.

Early whaling ships like the imaginary *Pequod* in the novel *Moby Dick* would take the blubber, the thick outer coat of the whale's body that is full of fat and "try" or render the blubber to remove the oil. This oil was used for lamps to light homes in 19th century America. But whale oil was replaced by kerosene obtained from petroleum and the kerosene in turn by the electric lamp. Today, the *Yoshino Maru's* crew only sliced the blubber and meat into chunks and froze it for processing and sale in the meat markets of Japan. Whale meat is considered an ancestral delicacy in Japan, part of a thousand year old custom of eating marine mammals that not only includes whales, but also dolphins.

A month later, she is deep in the Southern Ocean that surrounds Antarctica; this is where the Minke whales are found that will be killed.   Minke whales come here because this is where their food is, the small crustaceans known as krill.   One of the catcher trawlers, the *Toshi Maru* No. 25, sights its prey. The catcher trawler, the size of a good size fishing vessel, is faster than the *Yoshino Maru* and is a boat that could be described as a perfect killing machine. Her entire design is devoted to finding and killing whales. Her bow has an extension known as the "gunner's bridge" where the harpoon gun is mounted. The gun fires a harpoon that has an explosive charge. After striking the whale and sinking deep into its body the charge explodes. Barbs help hold the shaft of the harpoon in the whale's flesh and a line attached to the harpoon shaft and also secured to a reel on the catcher ship keeps wounded whale from escaping.

On the surface with her calf, the mother Minke whale knows that they are in danger. The Minke is not the largest of whales, only about 25 feet long at maturity and only weighing about five tons, but it is one of the most common whales found today. It is common, because it was too small to be hunted in the heyday of whaling that ran from 1850 to 1950. It was in this time that the larger right, sperm, fin, and blue whales were hunted to the point of extinction. Even its name echoes its small size. Meinke (later changed to Minke) was an 18th-century Norwegian whaler; infamous for exaggerating the size of the whales he had caught. His fellow whalers began to refer to all small whales as "Minke's whales". Eventually, it was formally adopted as the name for this common species. Even an animal the size of a whale is dwarfed by the vastness of the sea. In the needle in a haystack game that hunting for marine animals often is, the odds favor that the most common organism will be found first. And so it happened that these unlucky creatures were detected by the sonar of the catcher ship that ranged out from the *Yoshino Maru* in search of prey.

The whale dove deep, but the relentless pinging of the sonar found her and confused her. She stayed close to her calf. She knew that this was what she had to do and the best of what she had to do. Down and down she dove; but finally she knew she would have to surface. Minke's can only dive for 20 minutes or so—this also makes them easier to catch. In fear she rose through the blackness; the waters lightened and she could see her calf beside her, rising faithfully with her. She whistled-- warning the other whales in the pod. The sound would carry for tens of miles through the water. She surfaced and could now see the pursuer. They could see her.

Masashi Takano, a young crewman in his third year of whale hunting, smiles as he sees the whale surface. Warmly clad in a slicker with layers of clothing, he is the harpooner for today. His long black hair blows in the cold Arctic. He is a handsome young man, well liked by his crewmates and by the women of his homeport of Shimonoseki. The ride in the catcher boat is rough and he has tied himself to the railing of the harpoon pulpit that extends out over the bow of the ship to keep from being thrown in the icy water. He swiveled the gun toward the whale. The whale is bouncing in the sight of the harpoon gun as the boat draws ever closer. He is on the whale now. He pulls the trigger. A puff of smoke erupts from the gun followed by a long line. The harpoon hits the whale. She feels it go deep into her insides. Masashi is exultant with the blood lust of the hunt; he has harpooned the first whale of the season.

The harpoon explodes deep within the whale's body. In overwhelming pain, the whale is stunned and thrashes helplessly. But she is not dead. The power winch pulls on the cable attached to the exploded harpoon anchored deep in her back. Inexorably it pulls the whale toward the catcher boat. Reeled in like a gigantic fish, the whale's blood stains the water. She cannot scream—her pain is mute. Her baby swims frantically around the mother, frightened by the explosions, the thrashing, and her blood. The mother makes no more sounds. No more sonar clicks; she whistles no more; her songs are silent. She is winched up to the side of the catch boat and secured—another whale is dead.

The baby whale swims forlornly around the boat, looking for her mother. The catcher boat drives on, oblivious to the fate of the baby. Its sonar continues to ping looking for more victims.

The Australian news helicopter that had come from the chartered ship recorded the entire kill. They had come on a chartered vessel from Perth in hopes of filming the annual confrontation between the environmentalists and the whalers, but the environmentalists had not yet arrived and were only now in the port of Hobart, Tasmania. Oceanwarriors, the worldwide activist environmental organization had harassed the Japanese whaling fleet for years with little real success, but they had publicized the killing of the whales by the Japanese. The news people's budget for the charter would probably run out before the environmentalist's fleet could arrive at the scene of the hunt, so they tried to get as good a footage as they could. As the helicopter neared the *Yoshino Maru*, a powerful water cannon blast sprayed across its windscreen. The pilot yelled to the cameraman and reporter that they were heading back—if they crashed in these seas, they would be dead in minutes from the cold even if they survived the crash. The cameraman gave "thumbs up", signifying he'd gotten good footage of the kill. The helicopter beat its way back to its support ship. The *Yoshino Maru* and her catcher boats were left in peace to continue their harvest of whales.

Chapter 2

Bwana Doc

"Man's ethics must not end with man, but should extend to the universe. He must regain the consciousness of the great chain of life from which he cannot be separated. He must understand that all creation has its value... Life should only be negated when it is for a higher value and purpose -- not merely in selfish or thoughtless actions."--Albert Schweitzer

N**** N******** was at the Hyde Park Bar & Grill in Austin, Texas. It was mid afternoon. A cold January day, it had been raining and everything outside was still wrapped in a glistening skin of water, sparkling new and clean. The Hyde Park would have been a dark, smoky place if you could smoke there, but since you can't, it isn't. It is, however, still a snug, cool and a pleasant den to come into after a day fighting your way through the urban jungle of traffic that Austin had become. Built in an old house in an area close to the university, it oozed comfort while producing great fries and chicken fried steak. A brightly colored collection of art dotted its hardwood walls. Rotated out regularly, this series was a progression of people painted in odd juxtapositions to one another. In one a couple was lounging in a large tree; in another, two women occupied the cab of a pickup truck with oversized, jacked-up wheels. The restaurant was filled with the usual mid afternoon mix of university people and slacking state employees taking an early day off. He came looking for his favorite martini, made dirty and up with Monopolowa vodka, and sat down at his usual corner stool at the bar.

D. R. Schneider

His favorite bartender greeted him warmly, "N****, "How's it going?"

"No complaints, no complaints, Bravo." replied N**** N******* in a booming voice with a vaguely Central European accent. He was only known to his confederates as Bwana Doc. A tall, thin man with blue eyes the color of the deep ocean, and his coal black hair going gray at the temples, his skin was permanently tanned by the weather and laugh lines crinkled around his eyes as he smiled at Bravo. He moved with intent, not a casual air about him. To the rest of the world, he was a man few people knew much about. Known to people as N**** N*******, he was thought by many to be a retired computer entrepreneur. He kept a low profile and was seldom seen about town.

Bravo was a fixture at the HPB&G—bartending since its opening 20 years before. Bravo was a bald, tall, muscular man who did rock climbing in his off time. His keen intelligent face had been a witness to a thousand tragedies and joys told at his shiny copper topped bar. He enjoyed bartending for several reasons, the money wasn't bad, he could set his own schedule, and it gave him time to run his home business of buying and selling collectible cars on the Internet.

Bravo put N**** N*******'s martini in front of him as he sat watching the little flat screen TV that, after months of lobbying by the regulars, the management had finally put in over the back long side of the gleaming golden red bar. The story from the Australian broadcast company about the Japanese whalers came on the news.

N**** N******* had of course known the horrors of whaling for many years, but the graphic footage riveted both men's attention. Bravo spoke first, "Did you ever see anything more horrific?" N**** N******* nodded slowly, taking in the butchery of the mother whale and the thrashing of its calf, "I have, but this is the worst in a long time." Silence followed. This was the kind of comment Bravo had come to expect from N****. He knew there was much to his friend that he did not know and never would know. Bwana Doc's long lithe frame was rigid, his keen ocean blue eyes fixed on the screen, his dark tanned face still as he took in the broadcast.

The commentator was still droning on about the whale killing. N**** N******* looked at the picture of the little whale the way a next of kin might identify a body in a morgue. "How can someone kill, much less eat, such a magnificent animal?" he said more to himself than to Bravo. "Killing something like that for food." He muttered under his breath. His blue eyes squinted to slits, barely letting any light in at all. A stream of water from a high-pressure fire hose hits the news helicopter, blurring the video image. The helicopter swirled away and the image was lost.

Bravo didn't know what to say and doing what bartenders did best, kept silent, just nodding and making small sounds of agreement as he polished a glass vigorously, his muscular forearms bulging from the work. You get a lot of people in Austin that are overly concerned about almost everything from bats to unkneaded bread, to the crisis in the Somalia dust mite population, but this was different. Standing across from N****, he felt his emotion like a physical force. He had seen this in N**** before and it usually presaged an extended absence from the bar. Besides missing his friend, N**** was a very good tipper, so Bravo was concerned.

N**** N******* suddenly seemed to forget about the broadcast and turned his full attention to the woman who had been watching the broadcast as well and was seated one seat over from him. He soon had her talking away about herself. N**** N******* had a talent for making people feel comfortable about themselves when he was around. Bravo had seen this happen many times. As far as women, though, N**** never had any further contact with the women with whom he struck up conversations. He seemed a monk as far as the opposite sex. Sometimes, he would come in with some friends, always the same ones more or less, and they would then sit at a table and hold quiet intense conversations. He never introduced Bravo to these friends, but would always have a kind word and a nod to Bravo when he came in with them.

After a half hour or so of chatting with the lady and Bravo, he said, "Well, it's time to do something about the whales—I need to go." Bravo and the lady thought it an odd way to end a bar visit. Everyone has their story in a bar and eccentricity was a way of life for many in Austin. He hoisted his tall frame up off the stool and rocked his way to the brightly lit door and out into the rain-cleaned air of a late fall day in Austin, redolent with the smell of pecan and hackberry tree leaves turning to mulch on the ground. He had a sailor's gait—something a landsman like Bravo wouldn't have recognized.

N**** N******* was a great deal more than appearance presented. Not a middle aged entrepreneur, N**** N******* was a man on a mission to save the environment where governments and individuals had failed. He was Bwana Doc, already known for his exploits in saving animals and habitats that many had felt were doomed. Named for his exploits in fighting the plagues in Africa, his methods were extreme and not always legal, but they were effective. With the resources that vast wealth gave him, he would take any measure to save environment from the depredations of corporations and governments. Anonymous to the authorities, his previous activities were but a prelude to the magnitude of action he was about to take to save the whales.

D. R. Schneider

Chapter 3

Decisions and Plans

"What you can do or think you can, begin it—boldness has genius, power and magic in it."--Johann Wolfgang von Goethe

Bwana Doc left the HPB&G and got into his 1981 Series III Diesel SWB Hardtop Land Rover. Faded to the blue of a cloudy December day sky in Wisconsin, and more than slightly battered by what were clearly well off the road adventures, the almost antique vehicle was powered by biodiesel and had been his steadfast companion on many an adventure. Famously described as being "faster than molasses, but slower than ketchup", it was no car for the freeway, but was good for motoring around town to his various hangouts and to meet with his confederates. Driving to his lake front estate in Tarrytown in west Austin, he continued thinking about what could be done to save the whales. Blessed with a lack of scruples and vast resources of money to fund his plans, he knew something could be done that would be concrete, effective, and discrete. He knew, as so many people knew, that government intervention by laws was ineffective. Environmental organizations from mainstream to most radical had proven equally ineffective. Marine mammals had been protected in the United States and in many other countries worldwide since the 1970s, but the slaughter of whales on the high seas by Japan went on.

D. R. Schneider

Tarrytown was a perfect location for Bwana Doc to maintain his anonymity. His neighbors were lawyers, physicians and professors so self absorbed that they gave little thought to the man behind the gates of his estate and the fact that he might be something very different than the average denizen of their neighborhood. If they wondered at all, they thought of him as old Austin money that was living a low key life and enjoying Austin's live music scene or outdoor activities. His heavily wooded multi-acre estate fronted on Lake Austin, which also offered an opportunity to disguise certain other of his activities. He opened his remotely controlled gates to his estate, drove through grounds studded with ancient and gigantic live oak and pecan trees along a road lined with Italian funeral cypress. With a sharp left in the road immediately upon entry, nothing of the contents of the estate could be seen from the road. The fencing of the estate left it equally secure—tall stone walls studded with broken glass and razor wire artfully disguised behind a cast iron screen on top of the wall. Discrete monitors and motion sensors completed the wall's embellishment. He garaged the Land Rover in the attached four-car garage. His home was a large, low rambling stucco ranch style home with a tile roof studded with solar panels and an anomalous circular tower on one end with a wind turbine on top. It flapped slowly and silently in the slight wind. The estate was large and extended all the way to the lake made from the dammed Colorado River. Walled, heavily treed and hedged, it was virtually impossible to see or hear any activity from any of the distant neighboring houses or the street. Walking in

14

from the garage through his breezeway, he bypassed his large open living area furnished with masses of comfortable leather and the trophies of his various adventures, and went immediately to his study and sat down at his desk. Carved from the timbers of a wrecked clipper ship, it was an impressive mass of dark wood that still gave off the tang of the sea on those warm evenings when he opened his windows and let the winds over Lake Austin wash its rich mix of lake water and tree odors through his office.

His dog Banshee strolled into his office. Banshee, an English mastiff, was his steady companion when at home. Gigantic, aloof and quiet, she settled down at Bwana Doc's feet for her late afternoon snooze with her favorite person. Bwana Doc's cat, Oman, a large orange tabby looked up with disdain from his usual perch on an office chair and settled back to sleep.

The ceiling fan thrummed softly as he sat thinking. He knew that the whaling industry of Japan was a marginal one. Like many fisheries, it was subsidized by the host government and could not withstand a significant economic loss. Also, the number of countries participating in any kind of whaling was equally limited. Japan, Iceland and Norway were the only serious committed whaling nations, but their respective governments also supported these whaling operations. The International Whaling Commission or IWC, the official protector and regulator of whaling, had tried to stop all commercial whaling in 1982, and failed. In recent years, the support among the member nations of the IWC had eroded in part because the three whaling nations had influenced many of the small island nations that were members of the IWC, causing them to vote against a complete ban on whaling. Governments like Japan could say they just conducted "scientific" whaling, but the killing went on. Norway and Iceland didn't even bother with that nicety. They just killed as many as they wanted using loopholes in the IWC regulations to permit their activities.

The walls of his study were crammed with books and more trophies of his years of environmental and humanitarian adventure. Diplomas and awards from a number of countries completed the covering of the free wall space. A narwhal tusk crowned the unused fireplace, and a pair of .44 bore Joseph Lang dueling pistols in perfect condition flanked it on either side. Above the narwhal tusk was a plaque with a quote from Ross Perot, "The activist is not the man who says the river is dirty. The activist is the man who cleans up the river." The narwhal tusk was a gift from the Inuit peoples for a service rendered many years ago—another story for another time.

He opened his notebook computer and began writing an email using a special encrypted account. He was specific in his requirements, but no limit was set on the funds that could be spent. Bwana Doc had vast wealth at his disposal. He knew he would not receive a reply for the next few days, but Ali Mohammed Gamali, his dealer in "special" items would find what he was looking for if such a thing existed. Having sent his emails, he then turned his attention to dinner. His loyal houseboy and cook, Sarapand, had prepared him a simple meal of eggplant croquettes, and an orangejicama salad with a glass of Smithwick's ale.   Afterwards, Bwana Doc went for a long run in the neighborhood with Banshee, his mind working the entire time.

With the project underway, Bwana Doc decided to make a visit that evening to his friend, Mr. G.   A short, muscular jolly man with a head of short, curly gray hair that covered his head like an Augustan emperor, he was a frequent participant in Bwana Doc's adventures, combining the laid back lifestyle of a good old boy Texan with a lust for adventure.   Mr. G was a retired Air Force fighter pilot who had decided that he needed a more exciting career in an early retirement from the commercial airplane industry. Widowed by a tragic plane crash, he mourned for his lost wife and had never remarried. Now he owned a thriving music equipment rental and supply business for the live music industry in Austin. He had met Bwana Doc by chance on one of his earlier adventures on the coast of Florida and they had become close friends and partners in righting the wrongs of government and corporate environmental neglect and destruction. Besides a skilled pilot, he was also a great bartender, and someone who could talk anything out of anybody in any country in the world; he had a natural gift for gab.

Homeless Pete, another confederate, was called to join them at Mr. G's home that evening. Homeless Pete wasn't really homeless although he had been. A veteran of the Middle Eastern wars and a former Special Forces sergeant, he had been rescued from the streets of Austin by Bwana Doc.   Overcoming his posttraumatic stress disorder and drug abuse through Bwana Doc's expertly provided medical care; he had become one of Bwana Doc's most loyal and capable lieutenants. Skilled in a variety of lethal techniques and weapons, he could pilot any plane or boat in Bwana Doc's fleet. A burly man of average height with closely cropped dark hair now just beginning to turn gray on the edges, he gave an impression of imperturbable strength that was backed up by a considerable reality. He came over to Mr. G's to get some peace and quiet from his "family" of fifteen dogs, seven of whom were German Shepherds, reputed to be eating him out of house and home. He'd gotten a Ph.D. in comparative literature, and occasionally lectured at the local university. This allowed him plenty of time to participate in Bwana Doc's adventures.

Mr. G and Pete were in deep conversation when Bwana Doc arrived. They greeted him warmly. They knew that a new adventure was in the offing and they wanted to hear more about it. Bwana Doc related to them what they would be doing. The pair greeted the audacious plan with enthusiasm and the trio stayed up late into the night talking about what they would do to save the whales.

Chapter 4

Back in the Antarctic

"The real threat to whales is whaling, which has endangered many whale species."--Dave Barry

In jargon of Japanese whalers, the delivery of a whale to a factory ship such as the *Yoshino Maru* from a catcher ship is called *togei*. In this process, a rope with a small float at the end is thrown into the sea from the deck above the rear slipway of the ship. This slipway, a large door in the back of the ship that sloped down toward the sea when open, was the point of entry for the dead mother whale on to the working deck of the ship. A catcher ship crewman standing on the gun deck of the small boat then picked the rope out of the water. This was done using a *sumaru*, a line with a quadruple hook at the end. The line was then pulled to bring an attached steel cable from the main winch of the factory ship deck through the slipway gate. The lead end was then attached to the *oba* (fluke) wire that had already been secured to the dead whale. The line was then hauled back to the factory ship with the whale. Cables attached to the whale dragged it flukes first through the slipway onto the deck of the ship. The workers and scientists crowded around the mother Minke whale's body, their first catch of the season.

Hajime Hatamoto, the chief scientist, directed the work. Hatamoto was a member of Japan's Institute for Cetacean Research and had a long career in marine research. Starting with keeping fish at home that he had caught in the native rivers of Japan, he had been an enthusiastic mountaineer in college. After obtaining degrees in marine science at Ryukyu and Hokkaido Universities he had joined the Institute after studying dolphins for many years. The short balding man was an enthusiast for whales and whaling and had no sympathy for the people who wanted to stop it. He smiled broadly at his coworkers as they busily sampled and measured. A celebratory mood was evident. Wearing green safety helmets the scientists took samples of the diatoms and parasites on the whale's skin and the whale was measured and weighed. The ear plugs were removed using a gruesome coring tool.

The ear plugs were the principal means of determining the age of baleen whales. By counting the lamina or layers in the ear plug after they had been sectioned, an accurate estimation of the whale's age could be made. This was not how it was done on toothed whales such as the sperm whale where the number of layers of enamel in the tooth was used to determine age. The gunners on the catcher trawlers had to be careful to avoid hitting both the ear area as well as the bulk of the meat in the animal to maintain the scientific and commercial value of the whale. A clean shot to the heart was preferred, but difficult to do in rough seas. The harpoon grenade with three kilograms of explosive was a blunt instrument to injure the whale so badly it could not get away from the catcher. Even hit in the body, the animal was so large that huge amounts of meat and blubber could still be harvested. The mother whale had been hit near the heart and so had only taken several minutes to die.

Sometimes a whale might take hours to die and would have to be finished off by sharpshooters with high powered rifles—the ultimate in big game hunting.

A ceremonial barrel of sake was broken open with wooden hammers and poured over the carcass—a ritual meant to insure a successful season. After a quick toast, the workers began the bloody business of carving up the huge carcass. Long, sharp cutting tools called flensing knives that resembled long hockey sticks were used to cut the blubber into strips that were then peeled off using hooks attached to winched cables. The meat beneath was then cut off into chunks for quick freezing in the hold below. In less than two hours, the defleshed whale body lay starkly red and white under the leaden Antarctic sky, the meat and blubber boxed in cardboard boxes and stored below, ready for the fish markets of Tokyo. The catchers had not killed any more whales that first day; but the men were happy. The carcass was dumped over the side to begin its long journey to the ocean bottom where it would be digested over a period of months by marine organisms. The whale carcass would in fact be an oasis of life on the usually barren sea floor. Eel like hagfish would eat the meat from her bones and bacteria would digest the fat and other parts of the carcass. Even in death, the whale would support more life until her bones had been digested and sank into the sea floor around them, leaving no trace of her existence.

The men hosed down the deck and cleaned their equipment and then went below to clean themselves off and get out of the freezing air. The equipment of the ship was working well and the team of workers and scientists had done well together today. The teamwork so important to the Japanese culture was fully evidenced by their speedy dispatch of the whale's body. The prospects looked bright for another successful season—despite the annoying news helicopter. The long Antarctic summer made work easy—there were only a couple of hours of twilight a day at this time of the year. The usual environmental protesters were delayed and with any luck might miss the season all together. Life was good killing whales.

Chapter 5

Pirates Part 1

"All business sagacity reduces itself in the last analysis to judicious use of sabotage"--Thorstein Veblen

It was a bright sunny afternoon in the Wellington, New Zealand harbor. Oceanwarriors' five boats all lay anchored near one another on the piers not far from Queens Wharf, the center of the harbor activity. Every year, the Oceanwarriors' vessels would confront the Japanese whaling fleet. Delayed this year by a variety of difficulties, they were late in their usual harassment of the whaler's seasonal activity. Different approaches were taken to harass the whalers. Sometimes they would attempt to get between the catcher boats and the whale being chased. In the past, they had thrown butyric acid stink bombs that had smelled of rancid butter and also smoke bombs on both the *Yoshino Maru* and the catcher boats. Once they had tried to yank a harpoon gun from the bow of one of the catcher boats. Flying no flag, they were considered pirates by the Japanese. Roane Sander was a veteran of these confrontations; he had first gone along ten years ago as an engine mechanic and had gradually risen in the ranks until he was now the commander of the small flotilla. Oceanwarriors was composed of members from other environmentalist organizations who had grown dissatisfied with the results obtained so far in stopping the whaling.

Like the Japanese, many other countries regarded them as pirates and they were generally not well treated, but remained popular with a broad base of support throughout the world. Their actions had caused them to have their ships repeatedly delisted from countries' ship registries. Partly because of this, they flew no flag now, one of the marks of a pirate vessel. The crews of the vessels are also not on the friendliest terms with each other, making them perhaps more pirate like than they would be willing to admit. Verbal altercations were common and Sander was frequently required to settle arguments among the fractious crews. Many of the crew were along for the adventure and the unique lifestyle, and were perhaps not the most committed environmentalists. Their adventures had made them famous and notorious. Unlike his fellow crewmembers, Sander hated the whalers in his bones; he hated them as much as he loved the sea and the creatures that lived in it. The Japanese whaling was so pointless and cruel. His crews were a tool to accomplish his goal—the end of whaling.

Sander was holding forth on the *Edward Abbey*, the largest of the ships. He was lecturing his captains and their first mates once again on the need to keep the peace on the boats. A large, charismatic man, his long black hair streamed in the wind as he addressed them. "We are here to stop the bloody Jap whale murderers. We're here for no other reason. Fighting among ourselves solves nothing."

"A lot of us don't think we're doing enough, Roane." drawled Hank Kohler, captain of the *Extreme Environment* and a long tall Texan who had been with Oceanwarriors as long as Sander. He was along for the two women he was sleeping with—one on his boat, the other on the *Edward Abbey*. Women were drawn to the Oceanwarriors—they loved the heroic activities of the activists. It was much more fun than circulating petitions for the Sierra Club.

"I know, I know, but one step at a time. Every year we get closer. This is the most ships we've ever been able to get together. This year could be the year we get them to give up" replied Sander.

"You're the boss, but I'm just saying, we can only be together if we're really accomplishing something—then it'll be a lot quieter."

"It'll be better once we're at sea. Work will get people's minds off of things. We take on our last stores tomorrow. The next day we'll be off and after the buggers," replied Sander.

"What's this about a party?" asked Clare Wood, the only female among the captains in this supposedly egalitarian organization. She ran a tight ship. Her crew was mostly female and was exceptionally competent.

"Tonight!" said Sander with a relish. "A big donor is giving a party in our honor. "A full spread with band, drink, food." Sander was excited—there were always a lot of young wanna be female environmentalists who wanted to hear his stories of heroic confrontations with the mega corporations despoiling the planet. New Zealand was a very environmentally conscious country and extremely antiwhaling. "Now that is something that will get your minds off of fighting over strategy and bunk space."

"Who can go? We need to leave people on board to watch the ships." asked Hank.

"Don't you think the ships are pretty safe here in New Zealand? There are police patrols here in the harbor," said Barnard Hovenstein, one of the other captains.

"Barney's right. It's quiet here. No protesters. It's a law-abiding country. We need to leave someone on the boats though. Draw straws. Short straw has to stay on board," replied Sander.

The other captains nodded in agreement, all equally eager for the party after a month at sea. It had been hard work getting to New Zealand from their various locations in the Pacific and dealing with the range of problems that had caused their late arrival here. The superb climate of New Zealand was refreshing, but some socializing with new people would be just the thing to pick up everyone's mood for the voyage to the cold, rough seas of the Antarctic.

"And another thing," Sander added, "Captains and first mates are exempt from the drawing. All of you get to go. There will be a lot of dignitaries there and some other big potential donors. You can work the crowd."

"Who is this big donor who's throwing the party?" asked Clare.

"It's a big iron sand mining company—probably guilty over their pollution," replied Roane. Iron sand, a type of iron ore rich in titanium, was mined extensively on New Zealand.

If they had inquired further, they would have found that the company was actually owned by a Japanese company closely associated with Kyodo Senpaku, the company that actually collected the whales and sold the meat, and who funded the Committee for Cetacean Research in Japan.

Heywood Dowd was bummed out. One of the engineers of the "Edward Abbey", he had drawn the short straw. He had been hearing about the party for an hour before the drawing and was looking forward to a free evening on the town. He was generally disconcerted with the whole Oceanwarriors experience. This was just another disenchantment. He had been expecting days of righteous ecowarrioring, mingling nights with nubile ecomaidens, and plenty of weed and booze. But it had ended up being a lot of work. They had him in the engine room, helping the engineer—a small grouchy woman with permanently bad hair, a stickler for good engine maintenance. He had, after all, certification on several diesel manufacturers as a mechanic. The overweight engineer had a hard time crawling through the tight marine engine spaces. Hot and dirty most days, he was tired of the whole scene. Drawing the damn short straw and missing this big shindig up on one of the hills outside of town, ticked him off.

The light was just beginning to fade, commencing the long twilight of a New Zealand summer evening. Sitting up top, smoking a cigarette, Heywood looked out glumly over the beautiful harbor. A few sailboats were coming in from a day on the water and the ferryboat to Picton was working its way out to sea. The mountains rising above the city reminded him of the party he would be missing, deepening his depression. He didn't have a lot of appreciation for natural beauty, but suddenly he saw three stunning

27

Asian girls walking down the pier towards the ship. One was carrying a bottle and all three girls had drinks in their hands.

"Hey, sailor," the tallest one hailed him. "How are you this fine evening?"

"A lot better now!" exclaimed Heywood. "What brings you gorgeous things down here?" The large disheveled engineer didn't get a lot of attention from beautiful women.

"Well, we were looking for those Oceanwarriors heroes", trilled the striking woman, clad in a revealing red sarong. "We wanted to meet them."

"You're in luck, darlin'," drawled Dowd in his best country imitation. "Most of them are gone, but the best one is right here."

"You're kidding—and you taking care of this big ship all by yourself? That must be some job. You didn't get to go the party? Can you show us around?"

Dowd was only too happy to even though he failed to wonder how the girls knew about the party. The women stayed for about an hour, cooing over Dowd. Dowd gave them a full tour of the ship, such as it was. They stroked his ego and exclaimed over everything he showed them. Best of all, they left the pitiable, friendless ecowarrior the bottle they had been passing between them. The women wondered off to look at the other ships in the fleet. Dowd didn't know that the girls carried more bottles in their large handbags. Frustrated to see the girls leave, he would have liked to have had them spend the night. He would have liked to show them some real ecohospitality. He had to content himself with the bottle, and settled in to a good evening of drinking and watching the television available via satellite on the *Edward Abbey*. Soccer was on—his favorite. Visiting each of the ships, the throng of ladies made their rounds. While their reception was not quite so warm as Dowd's, the crewmen standing the watch were glad for the company and told to be friendly with the local people, which they knew, largely were against whaling.

Only one boat gave them trouble, a single idealistic lass who had been glad to miss the party, manned the *Rachel Carson*. Sandy Meyer had been an activist for many years and unlike most of the crew had been involved in the radical environmentalist, "Earth First" movement. Fit, tall, with gray hair, and a serious manner, she was a highly intelligent, fearless person who was not to be trifled with. The crew and her captain, respected her, and even feared her a little. She had dealt with being pursued by angry law enforcement and security men of large corporations when she and her colleagues had put sugar in the gas tanks of bulldozers or driven nails into trees so that the saw blades of the saw mills would be ruined when they cut the trees into lumber for houses. She was immediately suspicious of the Asian women who she recognized to be Japanese. The group approached in their typical ditzy manner that had worked for them with the other ships.

"What are you doing here? You can't come on board. No one is allowed on board," barked Meyer.

"No worries, little girl. We were just looking for cute ecowarrior men. We can see you aren't one of them," answered

29

D. R. Schneider

Tanazaki breezily. The women left quickly, not wanting to attract further suspicion, just laughed loudly among themselves and walked off into the growing dark.

Sandy Meyer snorted in disgust and kept a careful watch on the trio until they were out of sight and off the pier. She had seen that they had been to visit at least two of the other boats.

By eleven o'clock, the party in the hills above Wellington was in full swing. Earlier a bus had arrived at the pier to take the revelers to the mansion where the party was being held in an isolated area high in the mountains above Wellington harbor. Well fueled with liquor, Roane Sander had two beautiful local girls on either arm was regaling them on last year's actions against the Japanese whalers. The rest of the crews were similarly engaged—either in truly serious discussions with a variety of local environmentalists or like Roane, finding some companionship between long sea voyages. No one seemed to know who owned the large estate where the party was taking place, but they all agreed the party was one of the best they had ever been to. Excellent New Zealand wine flowed freely and the prawns and other seafood were exquisitely prepared. A wide selection of the environmentally conscious high society of Wellington was present. No one noticed a minority of Japanese gentlemen who seemed to stay in the background all the time, avoiding conversation with anyone.

At the same time, two black clad figures appeared along side the *Edward Abbey*. On their backs were compact Evolution Vision rebreather units for working underwater. The units recycled all the

30

air breathed by the diver and produced no bubbles. There was no sign of the divers in the water until they surfaced along side the boat. In a few seconds, they had thrown a line with a grapnel over the side, climbed it and were on deck. They moved quickly and silently. Heywood Dowd lay asleep in the open salon of ship, snoring in front of the large flat screen TV running a soccer match between Manchester United and Lyon, drugged by the liquor the women had given him earlier. The very same women from earlier had exchanged their revealing brightly colored clothes for skintight black wetsuits. Pausing briefly to smile down at the stupefied and overweight engineer and pick up the nearly empty bottle of liquor, Ami Tanazaki and the other team member from the Koancho, the Japanese Public Security Investigation Agency, descended into the engine room.

Swiftly they went to work on the engines, cutting essential wires and tubing. To top their work off, they poured a couple of liters of corn syrup into the fuel tanks. Unlike sugar, which doesn't dissolve in diesel fuel, the liquid corn syrup would be pulled into the engine and would caramelize in the heat of combustion to a gooey black mess, ruining the engine. Within ten minutes, they were back in the water. Similar teams worked on the other ships. Before climbing on board, they had also planted underwater timed contact incendiaries on the propellers and their shafts. On the ship with the zealous female watchman, they only planted incendiaries, but in retaliation for her diligence also put a small combustible charge on the hull, enough to cause a significant leak and take time to repair. Their orders were clear, they were not to sink the vessels, just disable them severely. Within a half hour, all the saboteurs were back at their own ship anchored in the harbor. A large luxury yacht, it had a moon pool open to the sea convenient for divers to come on board without being noticed. Once onboard, they silently made sail out of the harbor, by dawn they were well out of sight of land. By nightfall, they were well on the way back to Okinawa, the Japanese island that was their homeport.

Those members of the crew that had not stayed with the locals had made their way back to the boats at 1 or 2 in the morning and promptly stumbled into their bunks for a few hours of drunken sleep. They didn't examine the engine rooms and no other traces of the silent visit of the saboteurs were evident except a few wet foot prints, soon obliterated by the crew's own. The incendiaries went off silently at six in the morning, just as the sun was creeping over the horizon, washing the water with a beautiful honey light. They burned through the steel of the propellers, in some cases severing them. In others they merely burned through them enough that they would break under any amount of load such as a heavy sea or rapid acceleration. The other incendiaries burned through the steel hulls of the ships. As the crew rose from their slumbers, they still did not suspect that anything was amiss. The first alarm came from Sandy Meyers on Clare Wood's boat, *Rachel Carson*, who heard the water pouring in from the hole in the hull caused by the incendiary and the sound of the automatic bilge pump coming on. She reacted immediately starting the two emergency pumps and she was able to contain the damage. Rousing her drunken crewmembers to start the main engines, she began hailing the other ships in the Oceanwarriors' fleet on the radio. An engineer on one of the vessels discovered the damage to his engines and the alarm was general.

Roane Sander was nowhere to be found. He had been taken care of by the two ecobeauties that had latched on to him. Little did he know that these two were also in the pay of the Japanese and were actually high paid Wellington escorts. They had taken him to a bedroom upstairs in the mansion hosting the party and there he had been drugged like Heywood and left to wake up, sans cell phone and cash, by the two women. The Japanese knew well the discord in the Oceanwarriors' fleet and knew that only the charismatic Sander was holding the group together. The longer he was gone, the more his credibility would be undermined. Awakening about ten o'clock with a splitting headache, the badly hung over ecoterrorist stumbled around the now deserted mansion and down the street. He wandered down the road until he was finally able to flag down a delivery truck that took him back into town.

He arrived at the pier into a scene of organized confusion. Policemen were swarming over the vessels. The crew members, many suspicious of any authority figures, were unwilling to cooperate. A tender had been summoned on side the *Rachel Carson*, the ship that had been holed by the incendiary charge. It was keeping her afloat with an auxiliary pump. Sandy Meyer was in charge of that operation and it was going well. In the other boats, the crews had slowly become aware of the enormity of the damage. One crewmember had the foresight to examine the hull of the ship for additional charges—remembering the sinking of Greenpeace's ship the *Rainbow Warrior* by French agents in 1985. Free diving over the side of the boat in the chill Wellington waters, he discovered the damage to the propellers. As each boat was checked, the extent of the damage became apparent. The environmentalist's fleet was totally immobilized.

Sander was enraged. He ran from one ship to the other trying to establish some type of order. Finally he made contact with the police officer in charge of the operation.

"What are you planning to do about this? It's piracy, it's a catastrophe," he blustered, "we've been attacked by terrorists."

Recognizing Sander from press articles, impeccably tailored elfin police sergeant Emily Watson observed the red eyed, disheveled man reeking of alcohol with disdain. "We're establishing the extent of the damage, sir. Your ships are in no danger of sinking, thanks to the prompt action of your Miss Meyers. We are trying to establish the integrity of a crime scene, but we aren't getting much help from your crews. They've been all over the damaged engine rooms, destroying any evidence that might be there. And by the way, sir, your fly is open."

Sander redressed himself, blushing. "I'll get them off the ship and let your men work."

With the loud harangues that were his forte´, he bustled his crews off their ships and took them to a local restaurant where they

34

commandeered a room. There they proceeded to drink and eat themselves to placate their ineffectual frustration and fury. Ruthless words were said to Roane Sander by the other captains and crew. These were answered with brash denunciations of the Japanese that had undeniably carried out this nefarious attack.

Sander vented his rage on hapless Heywood Dowd. "What were you doing while these people sneaked on to my ship? Drinking, I assume."

Dowd was in a truculent mood and in no mood for his captain's self righteousness. He came right up to Sander's face. "Same as you, Captain—drinking—and not as much as you! I was drugged by these clever Japanese—what's your excuse?"

"Get off my ship you useless louse," barked Sander in reply.

Heywood backed up, looking like he was making room to take a good swing at Sander.

Hank Kohler got between the two men, seeing that things were degenerating into a fight that could only make the situation worse. Dowd wasn't popular among the crewmen, but at this moment he was more of a hero than Sander was.

"My engineer's been wanting to come over to the *Edward Abbey* and I'll be glad to take on Heywood on my boat. How about it, Dowd?"

"I'll be glad to join you. It'll be good to have a captain that thinks of his boat and crew first rather than going to a party," Dowd spat out the last words.

D. R. Schneider

Sander just turned away. He knew this was the easiest way to resolve the confrontation and he had bigger problems to deal with now anyway. He had to keep the group together—confronting the Japanese was more important than who his engineer was.

"Let's just don't forget who did this. I could have done better, we all could have done better, but this was a sneak attack of the worst kind. Now we have to all work together to get the boats fixed and go after those whalers before the season ends. Don't forget why we're here!

This partial admission of guilt placated the crew somewhat and they settled back to their food and drink. Sander was of course right. They'd look like fools if they gave up now.

Lieutenant Naru Shan of the Koancho, looked out from the Dockside Restaurant and Bar at the five vessels stuck in Wellington harbor and smiled into his Bruichladdich Scotch whisky. Bruichladdich was hard to find in Japan, despite the nationwide craze for the liquor. The Koancho was the Japanese public security agency, charged with both internal and external security for the country. The Japanese government had grown tired of the dangerous antics of the Oceanwarriors and had decided on some discrete preemptive action. The restaurant gave a perfect view of the environmentalist fleet, now guarded by pairs of policemen walking the piers. Although it was a little early for a drink, he felt he had earned it. He could still hear the environmentalists partying in the same restaurant. His all girl team had performed well. Although everyone would know it was the Japanese, no one could

36

trace anything directly back to the Japanese government or any of the companies involved. The Oceanwarriors would fear the Japanese more after this incident. They could have easily sunk the ships. The environmentalist fleet was stalled for at least the middle of the whaling season, perhaps longer. Shan sipped the fine single malt from the Island of Islay with deep pleasure. He rewarded himself with another round and then slipped off into the gloaming, ready to return to Japan. It was best to leave before the police investigation began to gather evidence. His team was good, but he had no illusions that some incriminating material might have been left behind. Forensic techniques were too good these days. His work was over for now, although he would return once the repairs on the ships neared completion.

D. R. Schneider

Chapter 6

Pirates Part 2

"There are only two kinds of naval vessels - submarines, and targets."--
Anonymous

Andrew Wattling was skipper of the cargo vessel *Perth's Lady*.
A young man, only ten years out of the Australian Maritime
College, he owed his advancement to both his wide ranging
competence, and his uncle that owned the ship.   Bluff, stocky, with
ginger hair, he was well liked by his crew and they responded with
giving good weight in their daily duties.   Three days ago, *Perth's
Lady* had taken on a cargo of rare earth metals at Port Hedland in
northwestern Australia.   Surprisingly, the small city of 15,000 was
the largest port in Australia in terms of tonnage.   Near large mining
centers for gold and iron, the discovery of huge deposits of rare
earth ores three years ago had lead to an entirely new metals
processing industry.   Used in a variety of specialty industrial
activities such as high strength magnets and high strength alloys for
airplane engines, the deposits of neodymium, praseodymium,
thulium, and other metals were much in demand.   Wattling had
some idea of the value of his cargo. He knew that his cargo ship
was to take the metals directly to the harbor of Shanghai and make
no stops along the way. That made for a tedious, if rapid voyage,
for the *Perth's Lady* was a fast ship for a cargo vessel. The mining
company had in fact, chosen her, because she was fast. His uncle

had told him that the mining company wanted no chances on the cargo, and they were to pause for no reason.

It was eight in the evening and a fine soft night like one gets in tropics deep at sea. Captain Wattling puffed contentedly on his briar pipe. The captain was finishing the second dog watch and waiting for the first officer, Scotty O'Brian, a garrulous New Zealander to show up. O'Brian was always good for a yarn before going to bed. Wattling heard a scream from the deck below. Immediately he turned on the flood lights on deck and sounded the alarm klaxon. Suddenly a trio of black clad men burst onto his bridge. "Pirates!" thought Wattling. He knew of the tales of crews taken hostage and held for ransom. One of the men clubbed his startled helmsman to the floor and then shot him. Panicking, Wattling attempted to make his way off the bridge via the other door, but was shot immediately in the back. The briar pipe clattered on the deck, spilling its ashes. No prisoners were being taken this time, no hostages. He could hear the screams of his men and scattered gunshots. As he fell against the railing outside the bridge, he looked out and in his last dying moments could not believe his eyes. Off the starboard side, a submarine was keeping pace with his ship and was flying a black flag.

Chapter 7

Whale Hunting

"The great whales belong to nobody and to everybody. In the struggle to exploit them the spoils go the stronger and the swifter." –Jeremy Cherfas

The hunting of whales goes far back in human history. It is likely that the same manner of hunting whales practiced by the Native American Eskimos of the northern western hemisphere at the time of European contact dates back to Neolithic times, thousands of years ago. Using their primitive skin boats or umiaks, they would throw handheld harpoons (made by attaching a knife to a mast) at surfaced whales and used inflated bladders attached to the harpoons to slow their escape. In some Aleutian Indian villages poison was used to kill whales. Aconite, a poison derived from plants in the ranunculus family was used by impregnating the lance head with the toxin. Once exhausted by the repeated harpooning and attacks, a boat would come close to the whale and cut into its side deep enough for the lance to be plunged through the outside coat of blubber into the internal organs of the whale. After repeated piercings, the whale was finally dispatched. After killing, the whales would be towed to shore or to ice edges and butchered. The choice parts were regarded as the flukes, lips and fins. The blubber (known to the Eskimos as muktuk) would be stored in ice cellars cut into the permafrost where it could be kept for extended periods of time. The meat of the whale was given to the sled dogs. The bone and baleen of the whales would be used for a variety of utensils including needles, scrapers, and even as structural members of tents. There was little waste—utilization of the whale body was almost total.

The earliest records of European whaling date to the twelfth century but it may have existed at least six centuries earlier. Interestingly there were little or no records of whaling by the Romans, although the 1st century writer Pliny referred to whale meat as good for the teeth. Like the Eskimo, Basques on the Atlantic coasts of Spain and France would catch whales in small boats in coastal waters and tow them to shore. In the seventh and eighth century, the Basques discovered an eager market for whale meat in Europe. The Catholic Church prohibited the eating of "red-blooded" meats on Fridays and holy days in part because it was associated with heat and therefore sex. Meat from water animals such as beaver, porpoise, seals, and whales were deemed "cold" and thus allowed. The Basques supplied whale meat fresh or cured with salt or smoked. Whale tongue was considered a particular delicacy.

As shipbuilding and navigation became more sophisticated and proficient, and as inshore stocks were depleted, whale hunters began to go farther and farther afield in search of prey. By the 17th century whaling was occurring off of Greenland and Iceland and even to the islands far north of the Arctic Circle such as Spitzbergen and Jan Mayen Land. As these areas were exhausted of whales, voyages became more and more distant. During the peak period of sailboat whaling from 1830 to 1865, the average voyage was two to three years. These ships, from 200 to 400 tons in displacement usually carried from two to four whaleboats. These boats were 25 to 35 feet long and had a crew consisting of boat header (usually a mate or officer of the ship), a harpooner and four to six oarsmen. Pay was good on a whaler. American whalers paid by the share system based on the total catch of the voyage. A green hand might get 1/175 of the whale oil and bone caught. A captain might get as much as 1/12 of the take. This share could be more than $12,000 a voyage and even additional was possible. Considering that all meals and board were covered in the cost, it was a good trade for those engaged in it, even if occasionally hazardous. Sperm whales might attack boats and even ships. They could also tow boats far away from the mother ship and turn the boats over, leaving the crew abandoned in the water.

By the 19th century, whalers were traveling to the Pacific from England and United States to hunt whales. By 1800 Nantucket Island and New Bedford Massachusetts became the centers of the whaling industry in the United States. At its peak in 1846, 736 vessels and 70,000 people were involved in the whaling industry. So successful were the Yankee and English whalers that the depletion of sperm whales resulted in a decline in the overall catch of whales. From 1850 on until the 1950s, the Norwegians dominated world whaling. It was not the depletion of whale stocks, but the inability of the American and English whalers to match the innovative technologies of Norway that lead to the decline of these nations' whaling fleets. It is probable that the higher profitability of investment in the businesses of the Industrial Revolution-steel-making and manufacturing, also played a role; reducing investment in whaling. There were still many more whales that could be caught, but it would require the speed given by steam power to catch these faster swimming whales. These were the larger rorquals, the sei, fin and blue whales—the latter the largest animal that has ever lived. While the use of whale oil for illumination declined, it still had uses in lubrication and for various food stuffs such as the production of margarine. The U.S. decline was rapid; the last whaling ship departed from Nantucket in 1869. The last American whaling ship sailed in 1928.

In 1864, Svend Foyn of Norway designed a harpoon fired from cannon rather than thrown by a man. He was not the first man to try this technology, but his harpoon, instead of a simple barb, contained a shell of gunpowder surrounded by an umbrella of barbs that upon entry into the whale opened and anchored firmly in the whale. The opening of barbs caused the discharge of a fuse that exploded the gunpowder inside the whale, causing a much more rapid incapacitation of these enormous animals. He mounted this lethal device on the bow of a small, fast steamboat, large enough to carry a winch that would haul the dead whale to the surface. Rorquals, like most baleen whales sink when dead. They lacked the large reservoir of spermaceti oil found in the sperm whale that made them buoyant. The exception is the right whales that float due to their thick insulating (and valuable) layer of blubber that is composed of buoyant fat. This was why it was the "right" whale to hunt. It could be killed and would not be lost to the ocean floor −it could be towed to shore or ship for leisure butchering. With the advent of Foyn's diabolical invention paired with the speed of the steamboat, the large rorquals could now be hunted without as much risk of losing the valuable catch to the seafloor.

In the 20th century, having killed off most of the whales in the northern latitudes, steam and diesel power allowed the last great whale fisheries in the Antarctic Ocean to be exploited. These held the rorqual whales, the largest animals on earth. Composed mostly of the Blue, Fin, Sei and Minke Whales, rorquals took their name from the Norwegian word *röyrkval*, which meant "furrow whale". Most of the members of this family of whales have a series of longitudinal folds of skin running from below the mouth back to the navel.   They had been spared in the 19th century because they could not be caught by the slower sail powered ships of that era. The Blue Whale is the largest animal ever found on Earth.   Up to 200 tons and 100 feet in length, this colossus of the sea like most of the baleen whales lives primarily on krill, a small crustacean found in incredible abundance in the Southern Ocean.

The slaughter in the Antarctic seriously began with the establishment of a whaling station in the far south Atlantic on the desolate island of South Georgia.   This became for the first part of the 20th century the world's largest whaling center.   Steam power and Foyn's exploding harpoon allowed the exploitation of the last large populations of these, the largest whales on earth.   Harvested for oil to be made into margarine, soap, candles, crayons and even dynamite, the relentless slaughter began.   Once whales conveniently located near South Georgia were killed, technological innovation allowed hunting to continue throughout the Antarctic.

The development of large factory ships with an open slipway in the stern of the ship that allowed the carcass of the whale to be harvested directly on board, allowed harvesting to continue around the entire circumference of Antarctica.   These large factory ships equipped with the fast catcher boats armed with explosive harpoons and helicopters to aid in finding the whales lead to the economic depletion of the whale population by the 1970s.   Many whale populations had been brought to the brink of extinction.   For example, blue whales are believed to have had a population of 245,000 prior to the advent of the fast steamboats capable of catching them.   Now the population is likely to be less than 12,000 worldwide.   Sperm whales, the whale of *Moby Dick*, were estimated to be 1,100,000 individuals before pelagic or open ocean whaling began. They were brought down to 360,000 individuals.   Similar reductions were seen for the Fin and Sei Whales.   Only Minke Whales were spared—their smaller size made them less economical to kill than their larger cousins.   Undoubtedly they also filled the environmental niche filled by the other rorquals which were also feeders on krill or did they?   What is the impact on the oceans of the loss of so many gigantic creatures? This is unknown, and it may never be known what else was lost in these devastating reductions in whale numbers.

It was well recognized in the early 20th century that whale stocks were being depleted. The beginnings of international efforts to manage and conserve whale stocks started in 1931 and culminated in the International Convention for the Regulation of Whaling in 1946. This Convention, signed by 59 member nations, created the International Whaling Commission or IWC. The IWC was formed to give advice to member nations on the management of whale stocks. It was recognized that many whale stocks were being depleted and some species were in danger of extinction. In 1986, the IWC entered a moratorium on all commercial whaling. As membership binds members to nothing except to observe the decisions of the convention and no penalties are attached if one does not abide the decisions, member nations can do pretty much what they want.

Norway, for example, still continues to hunt Minke whales legally while still a member because it has filed a protest against the moratorium. Norway feels that whale catching is a tradition for the country and should be allowed on those grounds alone. The Japanese hunt whales through a scientific permit from the IWC to study whale populations by examining their carcasses, but the meat and blubber harvested are sold commercially. The Japanese have made the argument that whales should be killed because they eat too much of the ocean's resources. They have developed statistics showing that thousands of tons of sea life such as krill, squid and sardines eaten by whales could supposedly be harvested for human populations. This was a justification for them continuing the

47

slaughter, which no international pressure could stop in any case. More recently, member nations of the Conventions have agitated for an ending of the moratorium arguing the need to exploit the whale populations for a growing world population.

Chapter 8

Pirate Hunters

"It is a very easy thing to devise good laws; the difficulty is to make them effective." --1st Viscount Bolingbroke, Henry St. John

Bennett Boyd leaned far back in her chair and looked out her window at the view from the headquarters of Interpol in the heart of Lyon, France. She was a striking woman, a tall, athletic brunette who wore her hair in a ponytail. Her lean and hawk-like face was fresh and good-looking, but not beautiful in a classical sense. Her large brown eyes were thoughtful as she looked out on the winter day, a swirl of snow blowing outside her window. She was a former commander in the United States Navy and lawyer that had served both at sea and in the Judge Advocate General's office. After leaving the navy, she had worked for an international security firm specializing in container terminals and port security. Recently appointed as the head of the new piracy unit at Interpol, she had thrown herself into her new job with enthusiasm.

Modern pirates had become a serious problem. Piracy on the high seas had grown during the periods of unrest in Middle and Far East. The collapse of the Chinese economy in the wake of the political chaos that had resulted from the civil war had spread the problem to the northern Pacific. The capture of a cruise ship by pirates, and the subsequent robbery and torture of several passengers had catalyzed international action. Interpol, the International Police Organization had decided that the growing depredation and sophistication of pirates and their now truly international scope, had created a situation that needed their assistance. Shipping nations had been instantly willing to donate to Interpol's resources, and this had led to the creation of Bennett's office within a month of the cruise ship incident.

She traced the pattern of attacks highlighted on her computer screen. The latest series of reports she had received from the United States and Australian navies indicated that piracy was spreading south from Malaysia and Indonesia into Australian waters. The pirate problem seemed to be like a Whac-a-Mole game where you hit the pop up heads with a hammer and they popped up through another hole. A prolonged sweep by the U.S. and Indian navies had brought piracy in the Malacca Strait—the hotspot of modern piracy since the 1990s under control, but now it seemed the pirate infestation had simply moved on to different waters. They had begun attacking ships along Australia's unpopulated northern shore and throughout the Indonesian archipelago. Reports of piracy were now heard of as far as the Bay of Bengal and the South China Sea. Aided by the civil unrest in Indonesia, it was clear that the trouble was spreading, not improving.

Pirates have been around for a long time and some level of piracy has existed worldwide even in modern times. The increase in international shipping in Asian waters with the demise of the Cold War and the growth of the various Asian economies lead to the increase in modern day bootlegging. Operating in their traditional pattern of using small high speed boats, they would board the victim craft at night, usually from the back of the ship. Their numbers might range from 10 to even 70 people depending on the size of their target and their motivation. In the past, the drive had been hostage taking and simple theft of payrolls and personal cash and possessions rather than cargos.

A troubling trend was the switch in the types of ships being attacked. Formerly local trading ships had been the prime targets. Now container ships laden with manufactured goods such as expensive electronics, or cargo ships laden with expensive raw materials were the target. Electronics, which could be identified rapidly through the microchips, used in their manufacture allowing at least some intervention to be taken at the point of sales, but precious metals and minerals once sold were untraceable. A resource hungry world would ask no questions in acquiring the raw materials it needed. The latest hijack had been an Australian freighter carrying rare earth minerals from a new mine in the Great Sandy Desert of Australia. A fortune in thulium, ytterbium, and praseodymium had been taken from the freighter, and it had been set adrift with the sea cocks open to scuttle the ship. Luckily an Australian frigate on patrol had sighted the listing, dead in the water freighter. By heroic pumping and quick action with a tow, they had managed to bring the ship into harbor at Derby on the northern coast of Australia.

The crew had all been found murdered except for the cook that had hid himself in one of the coolers. He was being interrogated. The task Bennett had was to find where the cargo had gone.

D. R. Schneider

Clearly the pirates had acquired a new level of sophistication and capability in not only capturing larger and more valuable vessels than ever before, but also in identifying which vessels to take and in fencing their cargos. Cooperation between all law enforcement authorities and the navies of affected countries was at an all time high. Her team was working with the National Security Agency in the U.S. that had satellite imagery of that area of the ocean. The attack occurred in darkness under heavy cloud cover and the satellite had not provided radar imaging of the ship. It did show the ship adrift during the following day, but no sign of unidentifiable or suspicious ships within a day's sailing range of the location of the incident.

Her second in command, Rudolf Delius, a diligent, precise German who had worked for years on the Russian mafia, walked in. "Any news on the latest hijacking of those rare earths?" he asked.

"Not much, we know where it happened, but the how is a big mystery. There was several tons of material moved off the freighter at night. They didn't take that off in speedboats. That's for sure," she replied.

The tall, almost cadaver thin German nodded in agreement. "You are right there. It was over 10 metric tons on the manifest. Expensive stuff. The thulium alone was worth over $50,000,000".

Boyd gave a low whistle and shook her head. "I didn't know it was worth that much. They certainly knew what ship they were taking. And a great cargo for a thief, totally untraceable after sold," Boyd mused.

"If it were gold, it would have been sent by airfreight or using a naval ship. I guess no one associated a metal like this with a high price."

"Well, the thieving pirates did, that's for sure," exclaimed Bennett.

"Any news on the new source we may have?"

"Not a word yet, he may not be in a position where he can try to communicate yet. We know so little about how this new group of bootleggers is organized. It's definitely a disturbing new trend. Just when we thought things were quieting down in the Straits of Malacca, then we get a cruise ship and major cargo ship hijacked within two months of one another, far outside the usual area of pirate activity."

The U.S. Navy had achieved a minor triumph that had eluded the Malaysian and Indonesian authorities. They had been able to place an operative inside what was believed to be this new pirate's main organization. Although they had not yet heard anything from her, they were optimistic that he would lead them to what appeared to be the largest, most sophisticated and secretive pirate group in existence. Bennett waited patiently for word from her counterparts. In the meantime, she spent time with her links in the Australian and United States navies establishing which of their assets would be available once enough intelligence had been acquired to pinpoint the location and nature of the pirate organization.

"The Americans are still sending that new ship of theirs down to Kuala Lumpur, aren't they?"

53

"Yes, the *Liberty* should be docking there any day now. Now that gives us some teeth to take out these bandits—if we can ever find them. We'll just have to wait for more news." Bennett slapped her hand on the desk. "Damn, I'd like to shut this new operation off before it gets any worse."

"We all would, Bennett," replied Delius, "The team has gone over the depositions of the passengers and crew of that cruise ship—pretty brutal stuff. They murdered a sixteen year old girl in front of her parents because they thought the father had money hidden somewhere on board."

"We're going to get those bastards, Rudy. We're going to get them," replied Bennett Boyd emphatically and with finality. "We've just got to keep working up the leads and wait for our break. The source may be able to contact us soon, too. Something's going to open up for us on these guys. You can't be that blatant and get away with it—there are too many eyes watching the surface of the seas, even though the ocean's a big place.

Chapter 9

Poolom Pannarang

"Where there is a sea, there are pirates"—Greek proverb

Like Bennett Boyd, Poolom Pannarang was also contemplating the view outside of his office window. But his office window was the porthole on his 30 meter yacht, *Labah Labah*, and it looked out upon a tropical island that looked hot and damp even through the window. Poolom lived on the ocean because that was where he made his living. He was a pirate. He had been a pirate since he was 12 years old. An uncle, who was already in the business, had given him a job as driver of a motorboat used to bring the pirates to the ships they attacked. He tortured his first hostage when he was fifteen and killed his first man when he was sixteen—a fellow Malay who had decided he should have some of Poolom's taking from robbing crewmen on a tramp steamer they had hijacked. By ruthless ambition, greed and intelligence, he now held sway over perhaps two hundred loosely affiliated men and women who had taken on the pirate life in the heart of the Far East. Recruited from the slums of Kuala Lumpur, Medan, Jakarta and a dozen other cities, they were as ruthless as Poolom and just as greedy. His activities had made him wealthy, unlike other pirates; he had not spent his booty on women and drink in the fleshpots of the cities. He had invested in larger and faster boats and sunk his money into other illegal adventures like smuggling, gambling and prostitution.

But his first love remained piracy. He liked seeing the surprise on a captain's ship when he walked on to the bridge with his black clad men and slammed his fist into his belly, letting him know that his ship was no longer his.

He pulled on his Montecristo Media Noche cigar and blew a cloud of smoke into the air. His black mustached face was hungry for anything. Just 30 and larger than the typical Malay, his long, well muscled body was covered with scars. His hard coal colored eyes crinkled around the edges as he thought of his latest raid and its extraordinary success. The bars and pellets of rare earth elements he had captured would bring over 50 million dollars on the black market. It had been a far better yield than even the cruise ship had been. They'd taken a lot off of her, but it had taken a long time to rob the casinos, the pursers and the passengers. They could have been caught at any time. This raid was over and done with in six hours. The best part was the rare earths were untraceable to him in any way once sold. Metal was anonymous once used.

His use of the old submarine to off load the bars-of the captured freighter had been sheer genius. He knew about the surveillance satellites continually watching the seas and he had often puzzled how to take the step from small motor boats that were relatively anonymous to something capable of holding a large amount of stolen material. The *Makuroro* had been the answer. He had bought the Russian "Kilo class" submarine from an African nation's navy for a token price and generous bribes. Beset by civil war and bankruptcy, the country no longer had the funds to keep the vessel operating much less pay her crew. Over 220 feet long and displacing 2350 tons on the surface, she could reach speeds of 25 knots underwater, allowing her to catch virtually any merchantman sailing the seven seas. In common with all modern submarines she could travel faster underwater than she could on the surface due to the hydrodynamic shape of her bulbous hull which made her handle poorly on the surface. Her diesel electric engines could carry her up to 6000 miles on the surface or underwater using her air gulping snorkel to power her diesel engines. Using her silent electric drive only she could still travel 400 miles completely submerged.

Now renamed the *Harimau*, Poolom Pannarang had had it refitted in India and had brought her to his island stronghold deep in the Lesser Sunda Islands of the Indonesian archipelago, not far from the steep sloped island of Komodo. The civil strife in Indonesia had caused the central government's authority to decay to such a point that it had little interest in activities in areas far removed from the population centers or oil producing areas of the country. Although relatively old, she was still hard to detect when submerged, and her dark hull was not that visible on the surface in the night. However, she could be detected on radar when on the surface. Even her snorkel used for supplying air to the diesel engines while submerged could be detected by good radar systems.

Still, the submarine gave him a tremendous advantage in capturing his prey.

This was not only because she was a submarine and one of the quietest diesel electrics ever built, but also because no one expected a pirate to have a submarine. After some discrete modifications in the Indian shipyard, she was capable of carrying a significant amount of cargo outside her pressure hull and also within the submarine after most of her torpedo tubes had been removed. She was the perfect addition to an ambitious pirate's fleet, whose largest vessel had formerly been the *Labah Labah*. He had first used her in the attack on the cruise ship, but had not allowed her to surface where she could be seen. She could be used to stage smaller ships for attacking merchant ships and could also be used to smuggle high dollar items such as illegal or legal drugs and expensive cargoes like the rare earths he had just taken. After taking on the cargo, she had cruised submerged to a small deserted island in Indonesia where the cargo was unloaded and would be picked up by its buyer.

He gave not a thought to the crew of the *Perth's Lady*. He had killed many men before, mostly his own which had tried to cheat him or challenged his leadership. Usually pirates took hostages in order to get a ransom from their families or governments. This time the men had to die because the cargo was worth far more than they were and because the secret of the submarine had to be kept as long as possible. He was excited by the possibilities it opened up to him. Already he was negotiating with a corrupt Chinese admiral for a second submarine that he could use for his operations in the Bay of Bengal.

His cell phone chirped. The text message confirmed deposit of the money for the cargo from the freighter in one of his Kuala

Lumpur bank accounts. He called his men guarding the cargo. "You can let them take it now—we've been paid," he barked into the phone to his lieutenant, Setiawan Perkasa. Setiawan acknowledged and replied his men would be returning immediately—no need to wait for the cargo's loading to leave and it would build trust with the buyer. The buyer had brought enough force that if Poolom had not released the cargo after the payment there would have been a gun battle. Neither side had a desire for that. Killing was done only when it got in the way of profit and the buyer certainly wanted to keep doing business after this coup. Poolom had placed sufficient armed manpower with Setiawan that no one would try to steal the shipment and payment would be made electronically to one of his Kuala Lumpur accounts after the cargo had been inspected.

As the sophistication and scope of his pirate's operations had grown along with his notoriety in the international criminal world, individuals now came to him with requests. Such requests were welcome. A buyer who wanted something badly enough would pay top price. The world's commerce paraded through the Malacca straits with over 200 major merchant ships a day. Although patrolled by both the Indonesian and Malaysian navies, it was the longest strait in the world used for international navigation and had many areas that could not be covered on a regular basis. And, of course, the use of his submarine opened up new vistas for his activities. Since he had begun operating off the coast of Australia, and had greatly increased the size and sophistication of his organization, his monitoring of potential targets had also increased. These requests though had created a need for greater intelligence gathering by his organization. It was no longer enough to wait for a ship to come along that was slow enough to be easily captured. It was now necessary to know which ships would be sailing and with what cargo. Luckily, he had found a person a couple of months ago who could supply him with just such information.

Poolom walked into the next cabin, where a young woman manned an elaborate computer and electronic console.

"So, my Jessica, what news do you have for me? Do we have more business?"

She turned from the console and looked at the tall, pirate. "We've got a couple of big electronic shipments from China that will be rounding Singapore in a couple of days and coming up the strait headed for India. Big fast freighters, not easy targets, but possibilities. I should have a full manifest in a couple of hours. Nothing off Australia right now. "

Poolom nodded, "Send me the courses on those freighters. You never know, one could have engine problems. We'll keep a watch."

Jessica Tate was his latest acquisition to improve his communications and targeting of thefts. Jessica was an expatriate Englishman with a talent for infiltrating secure communication systems. She was able to hack into the shipping manifests of all the major shipping companies. A fit brunette of average height, she had a hard, calm look in her intelligent brown eyes. Poolom had found her through an associate involved in international credit card fraud who had used her talents in his business. Due to an unfortunate accidental takedown of one of the associate's operations, she was now wanted for involvement in a variety of criminal activities. This assured her continued commitment to Poolom. His remote island base placed her far beyond the reach of the law. Her abilities were not limited to electronics and computers; she was also a skilled knife handler and had already dispatched one of Poolom's less savory and controlled thugs who had tried to be intimate with her. Poolom had found him with his heart cut out and castrated. Luckily he had had no relatives or close friends on board who might try to avenge his death. Now everyone but Poolom gave her a wide berth. Poolom was quite content—he knew that she could be trusted and her knife skills might come in handy. Piracy was not exactly the safest operation even for one as successful as Poolom. Three times his fellow cut-throats had tried to kill him. He stayed armed at all times and rotated out the crew of the *Labah Labah* regularly. Many were related to him, a further security.

Little did he know that the ruthless and trusted Jessica was an agent for the U.S. Navy. She was the "he" from which Bennett Boyd wanted intelligence on the pirates. She was not a native of England at all, but had been born in Sedalia, Missouri. One of the few women to pass the U.S. Navy SEAL program, she had been in Naval Intelligence for several years and this was not her first undercover operation. Formerly operating in Columbia, she had played a key role in breaking a drug smuggling operation using a shipping line as a cover. Highly intelligent, formidably trained, ruthless, and preternaturally calm, she relished a chance to shut down the latest pirate threat. She had seen the pirate she had killed execute one of their hostages by cutting off his head. She had no remorse from mutilating him, knowing that doing so would build her esteem with Poolom and make the crew fear her. It was like being a stowaway on Blackbeard's ship before his encounter with Robert Maynard. For her present assignment, the Navy had bypassed the corrupt Indonesian police that had turned in two previous informants that Poolom had summarily executed. They had turned the credit card fraud operator and had him recommend Jessica to Poolom. She had proved her worth early on by steering cargos to Poolom's speedboats. The acquisition of the submarine had been a new development that she had not been able to communicate to her superiors. Even though she had access to a variety of communications gear, Poolom had her and everyone else monitored by other crewmembers. She would have to wait until she was given leave to communicate this latest threat to shipping. The *Labah Labah* would usually head back into Jakarta or some other port on a monthly basis. Poolom had people he had to see in person in these cities and it gave the crew an opportunity to let off steam. She would just have to wait for an opportunity.

Chapter 10

Job Fair

"There is nothing more enticing, disenchanting, and enslaving than the life at sea." --Joseph Conrad

The bar was a popular hangout for sailors in Haifa. Near the port in the Bat Galim neighborhood, and located in the street floor of a moderately priced hotel, it was thick with the smoke of Noblesse cigarettes. Yuruham Mitzna stubbed his latest one out. An ex-submariner, he was waiting to meet a man about a job.

Peace in the Middle East had come at a price and ex-sailors in the Israeli Navy paid one of those prices. Even though never a large force, the highly trained organization had lost out when finally a lasting settlement was reached with the Arab world. Although no one on either side believed the peace was permanent, the lack of conflict and terrorism for several years had made it politically difficult to maintain the Israeli Defense Force at its highest levels. The navy in particular was seen as superfluous. Over half of her ships had been laid up or sold off, and that meant unemployment for her crews. With Israel's generous social programs and benefits, none of these people were starving, but most of them, like Mitzna, longed to be back on the sea. He had worked as a stevedore and in restaurants, but it wasn't the life for him. It wasn't the money; it was being able to be at sea. That was why he had stayed in Haifa; it always offered the prospect of going back to sea again.

63

D. R. Schneider

Wan Fu came waddling in, his hard eyes missing little. He was accompanied by his faithful lithe female bodyguards, Fee and Fan. Fee and Fan were classic Asian beauties, fit and intensely alert— their eyes missed even less. Dressed in vibrantly colored jackets, they carried an array of lethal weapons, none visible to the casual or even non-casual observer. The two were highly skilled in each as Wan Fu tended to go in harm's way often. Wan Fu was fluent in eight languages, and knew a ninth language, money, perhaps best of all. He was a born finder and fixer of whatever matter needed attention. Bwana Doc had chosen well and used him often for his missions. Wan Fu installed himself at a corner table in the bar, the same one he had been sitting at all week. He had put out the word that he was looking to talk to ex-navy men, especially submariners.

Wan Fu was quite open about his offer of employment. He was conceivably hiring a crew for a private submarine yacht owned by a South American billionaire. Privately owned submarines had become the latest status toy of the ultra rich and were every bit as luxurious as their above-water counterparts. Built with the same concepts as the ultra yachts of the surface, they would convey their owners and their guests underwater without the worries of wave turbulence on the surface. They were able to see the wonders of the underwater realm through large windows at their leisure as they traveled. Of course such a vessel needed a crew. Ex-navy men would be the best as the rich always have need of employees skilled in armaments and their use. The pay this hypothetical billionaire was offering was generous, almost unimaginably so. This was a sure enticement and it had worked well. Once the first few had come in, the word had spread all along the Israeli coasts and through the countryside. He even had men from Eilat in far southern Israel on the Gulf of Aquaba sending him resumes. He had enough men now to crew the vessel, but was still looking for a man who could be first mate or the captain of the vessel he had in mind. Perhaps today would bring good fortune.

Once Wan Fu had settled in, Mitzna approached the table. Wan Fu scanned the trim, middle-aged man carefully. Fee had already taken a picture of him with her mobile miniature camera and Wan Fu's staff was already analyzing it. It was unlikely that the Mossad, the Israeli secret service, would take any interest in his activities, but he was not paid to cause problems for Bwana Doc. He knew the name Bwana Doc was associated with actions in the past that would bring an unwelcome and unfriendly eye on his activities. An interconnected world of law enforcement and intelligence agencies did not make for a safe place for an entrepreneurial environmental activist like Bwana Doc.

Mitzna spoke first, "I hear you're looking for sailors, especially submariners." He spoke in English, accented, but well spoken.

"You heard rightly, young man. My name is Wan Fu. Have a seat." Wan Fu said in his high clear voice. Wan Fu invariably called everyone "young man" and his own age was indeterminable. By his looks he was ageless. He could have been ninety or fifty. No one knew, and he would never tell.

Mitzna took a chair opposite him and sat down. He looked carefully at Wan Fu and appreciatively at Fee and Fan, who smiled civilly back. Clad in slacks and partially open blouses under blue blazers, the twins were any sailor's dream of a great port of call.

"Who are your associates?" queried Mitzna, thumbing his finger at the girls.

"They are my assistants and body guards," replied Wan Fu.

"Bodyguards? They are very pretty bodyguards."

"Yes, they are, and extremely skilled. Fee and Fan are high-level practitioners of an assortment of martial arts, and they are very good shots. Don't ask for a demonstration. They have worked for me for several years, and I have never found their skills wanting. But enough of that, I hope you like beer, young man; I enjoy your Israeli brew."

Mitzna nodded and Wan Fu beckoned. A waiter brought over a couple of Temple Maccabee beers. The waiter knew the order was coming—Wan Fu's routine had been unchanging for the week he had been coming in. The two nursed their beers while Wan Fu laid out the proposal. As an ex-second in command of a Dolphin class submarine, Wan Fu wanted Mitzna badly and his loyalty to the project was absolutely required. Wan Fu began to discuss the positions available. He opened a thin folder handed him by Fee and pushed it over to Mitzna. It illustrated the submarine in cross section with a discussion of its technical properties. Mitzna was impressed with the submarine. "That's quite a ship for an individual to own!"

66

"My employer is a wealthy man, and he likes to appoint himself with the most contemporary and luxurious of possessions. He has several large yachts and sees fit to conquer the subsurface as he has conquered so much of the world economically."

"Well, the propulsion system is certainly one I'm familiar with and, as you probably know, submarines all over the world are basically all the same. They only differ in their power plants."

The Asian nodded in agreement. "Yes, so I have been told. I am not an expert in submarines. I am more interested in the people we hire. My employer is a man of many interests and he requires intelligent obedience and discretion above all.

"What do you mean by intelligent obedience?"

Wan Fu smiled. The Israeli was as quick as he thought he would be. "My employer does not like yes men. He wants men to tell him their minds, but they must be obedient to his orders, no matter what those orders are."

Mitzna looked levelly at Wan Fu. "I have only one thing that is above any order—nothing done must be against the State of Israel. The state is my home, my mother, not only of me but of my people."

"You have no worries. My employer is not of the Arab persuasion. And none of your work will be directed in anyway against Israel."

Wan Fu decided to level with the earnest Israeli. "Before you'll be working this boat, we have another job for you, similar ship, but a bit more serious and dangerous. Same pay, though, with an incentive."

Mitzna was intrigued, "Where will we be going?"

"Far, far from here, the other side of the world, in fact. And, I again promise you that the work will have nothing to do with the security of Israel."

Mitzna appreciated the honesty. Like most Israelis, his patriotism was absolute. Anything that would affect the future of Israel would be a deal breaker for him and would likely trigger a trip to the Mossad. But he didn't mind dangerous work. He'd done dangerous work for years, ferrying Israeli commandos to Arab coastlines and his reward was getting laid off with a minimal pension. This pay was good and he liked the idea of doing something completely different.

"I'm in. Just tell me where to go."

"You'll have a plane ticket delivered to your apartment tomorrow. You leave the day after." Wan Fu smiled to himself. Everything was going well. His crew was complete.

Mitzna left the bar. Wan Fu rose enormously, dwarfing Fan and Fee. "Ladies, let's return to our hotel and prepare for departure. Our work here is done."

Chapter 11

Bwana Doc Takes Trip

"Every person above the ordinary has a certain mission that they are called to fulfill." –Johann Wolfgang Goethe

Bwana Doc was picked up in the very early morning by a cab. A commonplace way for a person of Bwana Doc's wealth to be delivered to the airport one might think, but his goal was anonymity, not publicity. He was not picked up from his house, but from a luxury condominium apartment that he kept in downtown Austin. This allowed for maximum discretion on his part. Any casual or especially a non-casual observer of his house would think he was still in his Tarrytown mansion. Bwana Doc was careful to take all necessary steps to preserve his identity as a mildly eccentric, middle-aged retiree. He had no desire to live a life in hiding as he would be forced to do if Bwana Doc was connected to N**** N*******. Bowlin, his gardener, dressed as Bwana Doc in Hawaiian shirts, fedora and linen slacks, would drive the Land Rover out and around town a couple of times a week, completing the masquerade.

Bwana Doc left from the condominium parking garage with bags that had already been packed in advance. He always used the same cab driver—Moses Cantrell, a retired jazz musician who had injured his hands in a bar fight and who had been forced to take up cab driving for a living. Cantrell was still strong enough to handle

Bwana Doc's bags and he greeted his regular customer warmly as he stuffed the well worn Briggs and Riley luggage into the trunk of the car. The city was quiet in the early Saturday morning hours; downtown Austin still drowsing from the party Friday night.

Cantrell's Ford Crown Victoria with its floppy suspension mushed across town steadily and dropped Bwana Doc off at the general aviation section of the airport at his usual flight service with a comfortable sigh as it pulled up to the curve.

There he boarded a Gulfstream 450 painted an atypical greenish blue. His associate, Homeless Pete, was at the controls with Mr. G flying copilot. He acknowledged Bwana Doc's arrival with a wave as he methodically went through his checklist with Mr. G.

One of his seven German Shepherds lay in the jump seat just behind the cockpit, panting contentedly.

Mr. G turned and grinned back at him. "Your Hendricks's Gin is chilled in the bar frig."

The third member of the team hadn't arrived yet. After stowing his bags, Bwana Doc busied himself with turning on his laptop and establishing the satellite links with his field people preparing for the operation. They would stop in Santo Domingo to refuel and then cross the Atlantic to arrive at Praia in the Cape Verdes Island. The third crewmember entered the cabin. Preceded mostly by a long, slim, and elegant leg, a lady with the poise of ballet dancer, and the classic beauty of a Norse goddess slipped into the plane dragging a small Louis Vuitton carryon. Jaquelin Blain gave Bwana Doc a short smile, and an even shorter hello, and headed to the cockpit.

A no nonsense beauty, she knew Homeless Pete and Mr. G well, having worked with them on several other missions.

"Which damn dog is this, Pete?" she sniffed as she passed the somnolent German shepherd. The dog acknowledged her presence by cocking one eye open and thumping its tail twice.

"That is Bernadette—she hasn't had her vision yet, but we're hopeful."

"At least you didn't call her Medjugorje—we can be grateful for that." said Blain in a bantering tone.

Despite her beauty, Blain was the combat specialist of the team. Familiar with a vast repertoire of weapons systems, she was capable of mastering any fire control system in the world within a matter of minutes. Skilled in everything from hand to hand combat to the finer points of air to air missile warfare, she had trained in three services before "retiring" as a mercenary. Bwana Doc had hired her on a previous mission, and she had found his line of work more satisfying than supporting or overthrowing third world dictators. Working as a weapon consultant for a variety of armament manufacturers kept her up to speed on current weapon systems and paid her bills between missions for Bwana Doc. In her spare time, she raised Trakehner warm blood horses for equestrian competitions.

Mr. G. gave Blain a quick hello and turned back to his work. Mr. G was strongly attracted to Blain, but kept his feelings carefully hidden. This mission did not need any distractions. He knew that dangerous work lay ahead and everyone needed to keep his or her head clear.

"We'll have a meeting on the ground in Santo Domingo when we meet up with Jackie's combat team" announced Bwana Doc. "Let's get this plane in the air."

The greenish blue jet was shortly bound for the south and east. The jet climbed rapidly until it reached a cruising altitude of 30,000 feet. On autopilot, the crew took turns going back to talk to Bwana Doc, who was in a jovial mood. His confederates had noticed this in the past—when Bwana Doc had taken his first step on a mission to right an environmental wrong—no matter how challenging or dangerous, he would whistle, tell small jokes, and even burst out into short verses of songs or ribald limericks. The prospect of action always energized him. He knew that their crusade was just and their methods honorable. He was a pirate, but he sought no plunder, he was the man who would act to save those things who could not save themselves. He was the Robin Hood, not of the poor, but of those fellow inhabitants of the planet that we choose to call "lower animals" even they had been successful residents long before humans had made their abrupt and rapid ascent to the dominant life form of Earth.

They talked of many things; past adventures, the present campaign, old acquaintances that they would meet up on this journey that they had not met in awhile. Wan Fu and his ever-present beautiful consorts were always a source of amusement. The old Chinaman had their deepest respect; they had seen him pull off amazing feats of acquisition that had made their activities possible. The audacity of their present plan had really been made possible by the old gentleman's guile and persistence. He had worked with Bwana Doc for many years and, although well paid, he had told him more than once that he knew that Bwana Doc's work was the only way to save the environment. He had seen too much destruction in his native China. The loyalty of the confederates to the cause was complete; even if they profited from the resources available from Bwana Doc's great wealth. There was more to the future than just money.

Upon arrival at Amilcar Cabral International Airport in Vila Dos Espargos on the island of Sal in the Cape Verdes, they quickly cleared customs and took a cab to a private villa in the town of Santa Maria. The small fishing port with beautiful beaches was quiet. If anyone inquired, (a doubtful event), N**** N******* was here for a visit involving a lot of deep sea fishing. The Cape Verde's were famed for their sailfish and marlin fishing and N******* was known as an enthusiastic angler. Bwana Doc's activities had aroused the interest of the authorities in the past and one could not be too careful.

Jaquelin Blain's combat team met them. Four veterans of a variety of employments as mercenaries and professional armed forces, they greeted Bwana Doc and the team with laconic enthusiasm. Never ones for a lot of words, they spoke mostly with Blain, and sat in their own room in the house, preparing their gear. Their arms they would pick up later. Bwana Doc briefed the team on the plans for the operation. They would be in new territory for the action, not an unfamiliar situation for them, but the objective was clear and there was plenty of time to prepare.

Once settled in, the team established contact with their transportation. They had chartered a sport fishing vessel that was boarded at first light. Leaving the small harbor, few eyes were upon them and their behavior was not unusual. Fishing ships often left at dawn. The boat drove hard and fast far offshore throughout the day. Now well out of sight of land or any coastal shipping, they made their rendezvous at nightfall. A former oil exploration ship, the *Alistair Billings* had been specially modified some years ago for use in Bwana Doc's activities. The large distinctive derrick amidships that had been used for the well drilling operation had been removed. She now looked to the casual observer like a slightly odd looking cargo freighter. Her other modifications were less noticeable—among them were enlarged engines that had doubled her former rate of speed. Bwana Doc kept her maintained and ready in a Spanish port where she attracted little attention as she sat day after day. Her unique capabilities had made her useful in previous missions and she was a one of a kind vessel. It had only taken a few days to prepare her for sailing once their target had been identified.

The team was picked up from the fishing vessel while too far away to see even the name of the large cargo ship without binoculars. This kept the prying eyes of the crew from learning the identity of the *Alistair Billings*. The owner of the fishing vessel had been liberally paid to keep quiet and to stay out fishing for another week. He also had no reason to comment on anything he had seen as he hadn't really seen anything unusual.

Entering through a boarding port on the side of the ship, they enthusiastically greeted Wan Fu and his bodyguards, Fee and Fan. On board, Bwana Doc saw that all was in readiness for the next stage of the adventure. His contacts in South America assured him that everything was ready. The *Alistair Billings* immediately set sail for the south giving the Cape Verde islands and all other shipping a wide berth.

D. R. Schneider

Chapter 12

A Very Rich Woman Has a Very Good but Bad Idea

"A woman's perfume tells more about her than her handwriting."--Christian Dior

Renee Chevillac was a worried woman as she sat behind her large, baroque Louis Quatorze table that served as her work space in her office in the heart of Paris.

A short, adequately beautiful and elegantly dressed woman with hair that would be graying if she allowed it to, she was head of one of the most regarded and famous perfumers in the world. She had weathered many a crisis in a volatile business, but the problem that confronted her now had her stymied. She had found it growing worse for years and had finally decided that a solution had to be found or it was time to find a buyer for her company. The entire $25 billion dollar cosmetics industry had been floundering for some time. The problem was too many perfumes with similarities had lead to a destruction of brand loyalty. Customers would switch to a new perfume at the drop of a hat. Clothing manufacturers would promote their own perfume with the hottest pair of designer jeans and sales would soar for that fragrance. Women who would use Chanel #5 or Shalimar their entire lives were now rare.

That meant that it was that much more difficult to recoup the cost of developing a new perfume and promoting it. She had set her R&D department the task of coming up with a solution to the problem. She had told them there had to be an answer—and if not—they would no longer have their jobs. The meeting would be in a few minutes.

Her secretary called on the phone, "Monsieur Lampin and his group are here, Madame."

Her secretary was a well set up and intelligent young man. A very good assistant, he was also entertaining in other ways outside of the office. She smiled at the thought that maybe this meeting would bring some good news and they could celebrate tonight.

"Send them in, Robert," she replied.

Three people walked into her office; Mr. Nikolas Lampin and two assistants, one male, one female. Mr. Lampin was head of her research and development program. A forty-year veteran of the perfume industry, he was as skilled in picking women's scents as in blending them. Years of experience had made him legendary in the industry. He was a man who, like Chevillac, had overcome many challenges in his years in the business. A short, thin individual with a dry, dignified air, he habitually wore his white lab coat at any meeting at work. It made him distinctive from the packs of young marketers that crowded the ranks of the perfume company. Otherwise, he could have been a bank manager or an accountant. Many said about him that he knew the soul of a woman's nose, and that was the most important attribute of his job. He had cowed many a young employee by fixing his gaze upon them and asking the important questions. To a man he would say, "Does that fragrance make you want to sleep with the woman wearing it?" To a woman, "Does that fragrance make you feel like every man in the room is falling in love with you?" Madame Chevillac's challenge had left him confounded for a few weeks, but then he had hit upon an idea and put his youthful staff to work on it.

They filed into the conference room. Lampin did not use a fancy computer presentation. He had prepared a one page sheet with the concept of the perfume. After they were all seated, he passed a copy to Chevillac who, accustomed to this eccentricity, accepted it and sat and read it carefully for several minutes in silence. The other three employees waited nervously.

Her cool gray eyes looked up at the paper and stared at the old man.

"This is an astonishing concept, Lampin. It is every perfume manufacturer's dream!"

Lampin's normally severe face smiled briefly, "Yes, Madame. The concept is novel and the effect is quite remarkable. The user develops an addiction to the perfume, not as severe as one might expect from tobacco or heroin, but milder. They develop a habit immediately upon using the product. We have a short video to show you that illustrates the effect."

Chevillac was surprised by Lampin's use of technology. This must indeed be something special for him to depart from his usual way of reporting the status of project.

His male assistant, Philippe Renault, had synched his wireless connection to the projector in the conference room. The lights

D. R. Schneider

dimmed and a video of a middle aged woman and one of the assistants seated at a table began to play.

Lampin began the commentary. "This woman is being given her first sample of the perfume. Note the application to her wrist. We now leave her seated at the table. She has the run of the room. We fast forward to one half hour later. The woman is visibly nervous, running her hand through her hair constantly. She looks again and again at the door. Finally the technician enters. The woman asks him frequently for more perfume. He brings in the same sample box that he had earlier. She grabs at it, searching frantically. She thumbs through the box and finding the distinctive vial that he had used earlier, applies more to her arms and neck. "

"Remarkable, but certainly the effect is too strong. The users will become alarmed." Chevillac commented. She was impressed, but also cautious.

"The sample shown is full strength, by simple dilution we can make the effect less violent, still addictive but more subtly so."

"How was such a thing discovered?" Chevillac asked. "Was it an accident?"

"Not entirely an accident", answered Lampin's second in command, Gavrille, a middle aged heavy set woman, who had several successful products on her resume' already and was ambitious for Lampin's job when he decided to retire. She had every reason to want Chevillac's to stay an independent perfumier rather than part of a conglomerate selling sunglasses and panty hose. She worshipped Lampin as a true master of the art of perfume making.

"Monsieur Lampin remembered an incident many years ago when a new blend was tested on a group of women and they actually called after the testing and demanded more of the perfume. Subsequent batches of the same blend did not fare well in testing and it was never marketed. We decided to return to the original sample and retest it. The results were remarkable. Whoever used the perfume demanded to have it for several days afterward—a salesman's dream!"

Chevillac knew that Lampin was like a hamster and kept in deep cold storage under inert nitrogen gas every preparation the company had ever made. It was not an inexpensive procedure to follow, but he insisted upon it saying that perfume manufacture was never an exact science and that the original preparations should always be at hand to compare with samples from current production if needed. This had paid off for the company more than once in solving quality control problems.

Lampin took up the story, "We have analytical tools now not available to us when this original perfume was made. The mass spectrometer, the high performance gas chromatograph, and so forth. We analyzed the original and subsequent samples and discovered that it only varied in one component, found in only one ingredient."

"And what was that?" demanded Chevillac, anxious to know.

"Ambergris."

D. R. Schneider

"Ambergris!" exclaimed Chevillac. The finest perfumes were still made from the oddest of ingredients such as the musk glands of civet cats or beavers, but ambergris was one of the rare of perfume ingredients. Called by the ancient Chinese, "dragon's spittle fragrance," it had been used for centuries in perfumes, medicines, as a flavoring in foods, or countless other uses. Madame du Barry supposedly washed with it to make herself irresistible to Louis XV. Found washed up on the shores of seldom-walked beaches of the world, or floating on the surface of sea in lumps, it had the most curious origins. Born as a secretion of the liver of the sperm whale, it formed in its intestines as a protective coating around the beaks of squids that had been eaten by the whales. It was excreted in the feces of the whale. Over time it was altered by the sun and sea and turned from a soft whitish gray material until a hardened darkened mass exuding a peculiar odor that echoed of a sweet smelling wood somewhere. It was used as a fixative to extend the fragrance of perfumes and make them last longer on the wearer. Although synthetic ambergris components had been produced, ambergris was still sought eagerly by perfumers, and high quality material that sold for $10,000 a pound.

"Yes, from the belly of a sick whale comes a solution to the problem of fickle customers," exclaimed Lampin. "And therein lies the problem. The reasons that other batches failed to have the same properties is that the ambergris used in the first preparation had a unique composition. We lacked a sufficient quantity of the original material to make a definitive analysis of the structure of the one unique compound we found. We do know from our purchasing notations from the ambergris supplier that the materials used were obtained from a freshly killed whale, unlike most ambergris which is found as flotsam, floating on the surface of the ocean or washed up on shore. Ordinary ambergris of various types and ages has no effect—we have checked it repeatedly."

Gavrille took up the story, "Our theory is that the immersion or time out of the whale allows the substance to be decomposed or perhaps evaporate. That is why it was found in this fresh ambergris only," Chevillac's heart sank.   She knew the whaling industry was a thing of the past. The great fleets that had harvested the whales of the seas were all gone. Many countries even forbade any trade in the products of whales.

Lampin sensed her chagrin. "Do not despair, Madame. We have a plan to obtain a similar ambergris."

And then he began to explain his idea.

D. R. Schneider

Chapter 13

A Good Idea Cannot be Kept a Secret

"Three may keep a secret if two of them are dead."—Benjamin Franklin

Lampin's other assistant; Amelie Broussard had not been invited to the meeting. She was upset and feeling vindictive. Short, young, unattractive, and not particularly articulate, she had been Lampin's assistant for about 5 years. Lampin had chosen the old woman and his pet man to go to the big presentation, leaving her, the one that did all the work to stew in her office. Ambitious and industrious, she found the rigid office hierarchy of the antiquated perfume company stifling. Miffed at being excluded from the important meeting, she plotted her revenge against the old man and Chevillac. With no prospect of promotion until Lampin retired, and since she was not a favorite of Gavrille, even then she might not be promoted. She had decided that her ambitious nature should best be gratified by an alliance with a rival house. An assiduous attendee of trade shows and haute couture events, she had made several good friends in other perfume companies. As frequently as she could, she met them for lunch or for dinner. She did not suspect that one of these friends, Cheryl Bouvoir of one of their leading rival fashion houses, Vaneel, had cultivated her as a friend specifically with the idea that she might give out some information on Chevillac's products in development. Amelie had let her know already that something monumental was in development, but had been careful with her hints. She knew what she wanted. Amelie gave Cheryl a call. "I need to see you, the things we talked about before have come to pass. We need to discuss this personally." Bouvoir suggested a dinner at a nondescript bistro far from work where they could talk discretely.

Amelie agreed. They met for an early dinner at 8:00. It was a Friday, so they could spend the evening. Amelie related the nature of the new discovery of the addictive perfume.

Bouvoir was amazed by the product. "It can't be real!" she exclaimed in disbelief.

"I assure, my dear, it is very real. I even tested it myself. After one application, I had the need to put more of the fragrance on within 30 minutes. It was a craving like the need for sex. Extraordinary. It did pass and that was not unpleasant, an additional benefit in my mind. This isn't like being hooked on heroin. Lampin and Chevillac truly have a blockbuster product with this."

Bouvoir's mind raced. "So my dear, what is the secret?" she asked ingenuously.

"I can't say—you know how secrecy agreements are written. We can't say a word—in fact, I've told you much too much already," replied Amelie. "And you know how small our industry is. No one would employ me again. This is just a little innocent gossip, which will soon be on the street anyway. It's not an airtight business as you are aware."

It was clear that Amelie would not part without the information without a lot more enticement and that carrot would have to be financial.

"My dear, this news is simply too much for me to grasp. We will have to talk more about it. It is simply tremendous."

"Yes, replied Amelie, "Chevillac's company will make a fortune off of this perfume. It will make the combined earnings from Chanel No. 5, Shalimar, and Arpège seem like peanuts. It is worth a lot of money to know more about this product, she said insincerely. Amelie knew the worth of her information and Vaneel would have to come up with a healthy payment to make her telling any more information worthwhile. With enough money, she could start her own business or just retire to another country beyond the reach of Chevillac's lawyers. After all, it would be a hard thing to prove in any case. Vaneel certainly wasn't going to say anything.

"Perhaps we should meet again this weekend to discuss the matter further."

"I'm agreeable. You have my cell phone. You know how I love the fragrance business, I'm always up for profitable discussions," said Amelie, not wanting to leave any doubt about where she stood on the matter.

"I understand perfectly, my dear," replied Bouvoir. "I understand perfectly." snapping her purse shut and getting up from the table.

As soon as she left the restaurant and Amelie was out of sight, Cheryl called her boss, Henri Vaneel, the President of Vaneel

Fashions.   After hearing the story, Vaneel was immediately enthusiastic. Vaneel had always held themselves as the premier French perfume company until Chevillac had come along.   He burned for a way to bring his rival down and he could not allow this revolutionary fragrance to come to market.   Stealing secrets in the perfume business was a stock in trade as it was in all businesses. A new scent was scrutinized by sophisticated analytical devices and "reverse engineered" as a matter of course, but seldom could they be reproduced exactly.   The payoff from an addictive perfume would be so enormous, and if they acted quickly they could block Chevillac for at least a year from completing the formulation while they were taking the market.   He could once again be the dominant force in haute couture perfume.

"How sure are you of this?" he quizzed Cheryl Bouvier.

"I've been talking to her for a year.   She's Lampin's personal assistant and sees no prospect of advancement when he retires. She doesn't make a lot of money.   She's got access to the information. There's no doubt.   Give her a good taste of what we would pay her and she'll talk."

"Good, he replied greedily. "Let's move on this.   We'll pay her something this weekend.   I'll get you the money tomorrow.   Set up a meeting.   But get something concrete from her."

"It will be done.   I'll call her tomorrow early."

They met in the Luxembourg Gardens on Saturday afternoon.   It was a typical winter day in Paris with a dust of snow on the ground. Few people were about.   Two or three hardy mothers were pushing their robust babies about in prams in that relentless European belief that fresh air was essential for children. A few cold birds looked for a handout. The dry fountains looked forlorn with their coat of ice.

Bouvoir carried a valise with 400,000 Euros. The two women talked earnestly as they strolled about the cold park.

Cheryl wanted to know where they were getting the ambergris. "I don't know exactly but I know I've heard the Japanese mentioned. They are the only people still catching whales that might have fresh ambergris in their stomachs. Exactly how, I don't know. That is something Chevillac, or one of her people in purchasing may be arranging. But with my information, if you have the ambergris, you can discover the compound yourself. I have the data on the prior testing of the ambergris. You can reach the market first."

"But how will we get the ambergris? Maybe we should just wait until Lampin has worked out the structure of the compound and synthesized it."

"There may be many issues there, he may choose to patent it, he may not let me know the structure—he often compartmentalizes things, there are too many 'ifs'. And the whaling season is ending soon; there will be no other opportunities for more ambergris this year."

"I see, you are right," Cheryl said. "We must get the ambergris. We know clever and resourceful men—they will find a way. But keep me informed as you learn more information. There are more valises like this available."

Cheryl ended their conversation by handing off the case to Amelie. She was pleasantly astonished when she opened it after returning to her apartment. This was enough for a very good down payment on a nice apartment or even a house in the country. And it was more than she had made in 5 years at Chevillac. She would have to take the money out of the country, to Switzerland to hide it from the tax men. But there were always ways of using it legitimately in France once it was safely stored. She began planning a long weekend trip to Zurich. She would disguise it as a ski trip with a non-existent boyfriend.

And of course, there was the prospect of more payment if she could get more information.

Cheryl's boss was not entirely pleased. "It's good information, but how do we get this special ambergris?"

"I've thought about that. We've used suppliers for raw materials who were not as we say, totally legitimate. We've needed rare herbs from embargoed African nations, for example. They've always been able to help us out."

"A good idea. I'll contact them personally on Monday. We have to act immediately on this."

"What if we are unable to get the ambergris?"

"Then on all counts, the ambergris must be destroyed before Chevillac gets it. We must arrange whatever plans we make that we will have the option to destroy the material. I will discuss this matter when I contact our "special supplier" replied Vaneel.

Cheryl Bouvier warmed to the "we" in his voice. She had always been attracted to her silver haired boss and could only hope this success might lead to something more intimate. Certainly they were partners in crime now.

He did not wait for Monday. He immediately called his contact for obtaining rare and difficult to obtain perfume ingredients. Many of these came from war torn parts of the world that needed special skills to get out rarely harvested herbs or other plants.

Ali Mohammed Gamali was his contact. At the crossroad of questionable trade, he was the man one turned to when they needed something out of the ordinary. He did not connect this phone call with the earlier call from Bwana Doc. At first he was not encouraging, "Fresh ambergris from a whale—the only possibility would be a country killing sperm whales—perhaps Japan."

"We have information that the Japanese are going to be the source and may already be hunting for the whales. Perhaps you could obtain it from them by some means?"

"Very difficult, very difficult. It will be expensive." replied the soft voice with a surprisingly faint Arab accent. Despite his name, Gamali was in fact Lebanese and spoke not only Arabic, but also English and French fluently.

"I am prepared to pay 10,000,000 Euros for 5 kilos of fresh ambergris," replied Vaneel.

Ali Mohammed Gamali suppressed a gasp. That was an unheard of price for ambergris which typically might sell for less than $20,000 a kilo. "That of course will make things easier. A generous buyer can always find sellers. I will make a few phone calls. When would be convenient to call you back?"

"Call me at this number at any time. This is a matter of urgency!" snapped Vaneel.

After hanging up, Gamali sat in thought a while. Poolom had done well for him in obtaining the rare earths the German manufacturing consortium required for their new type of superconducting material. He knew that while the pirate was relatively far away from the Southern Ocean where the Japanese whaling fleet operated, Poolom now had the means to travel much farther afield. It had been Gamali that had brokered the sale of the Russian submarine to Poolom. He was well connected to the navies of the world who often needed or wanted to get rid of vessels in their possession. It was only one step from that to helping get rid of vessels that they wanted to keep laughed Gamali silently to himself. He made the call to Poolom Pannarang and explained the offer.

Poolom was intrigued. He had heard about the Japanese whaling fleet and he immediately put Jessica to work finding out more. In short order, she had narrowed down their position and through interfacing with a commercial land satellite operation and an email to an environmentalist website for the area that the ships usually cruised, she soon had an image of their position within the last 24 hours. There were few ships that roamed those deserted frozen waters.

Poolom considered the proposition. He had sailed the submarine from Africa and she was in good working order after the refit, and could easily make the journey which looked to be around 6000 miles round trip. He would also need some additional armaments to take along. While he wasn't expecting a fight, just as with the *Perth's Lady*, it would be better if there were no witnesses to report the presence of this strange submarine sinking a Japanese ship. It would be a long voyage back to the relative safety of Indonesia and he did not want a pursuit by any hostile naval vessels. The *Yoshino Maru* and any catcher ships that might happen to be around would all have to be sunk. Also, they could not be allowed to radio any information out. It would not be the most profitable venture, but his reputation would reach new heights. He would be famous as a pirate and no longer thought of as a mere petty ship hijacker. Most importantly, the local people would take notice. He would be viewed with respect and fear. As the chaos in Indonesia continued, he could imagine taking over several of the islands outright and starting his own country. He could indeed become the pirate king!

He called Gamali back. "I'll need more money for one thing. $10,000,000 and you will need to get me at least three or four torpedoes for the submarine and perhaps some hand launched missiles I can use against ships. I have to be able to defend myself."

Gamali smiled to himself. He imagined what kind of "defense" Poolom had in mind. The best defense is a good offense. He wouldn't want to be a Japanese whaler in a month or so.

"I can do that. I'll email you the prices once I get them. You can have them in three days, once I receive payment."

Poolom summoned the commander of the submarine to the *Labah Labah*.

"Prepare the submarine for a voyage of three months into cold climates. We will also be loading armaments."

"What kind of armaments?" inquired the wiry blonde haired Russian, Vladimir. A veteran of the Russian mafia who had served 10 years in the Russian Submarine Service on both conventional and nuclear boats before moving on to a career in crime, he had been a package deal with the sale of the submarine to the Africans. When Poolom had acquired the submarine he had been glad to come along. Poolom paid better than the Africans and was more interesting to work for. Africans were just interested in bloody nothing but shooting and sex. To Vladimir, it seemed that most of them had AIDS and were just thugs. Poolom had class. Piracy was an up and coming business with all the domestic chaos in the area. He liked the climate and the women better too.

"Hand fired missiles and some torpedoes," replied Poolom.

The Russians eyes widened, "Torpedoes? We got some big job, boss?"

"Yes," Poolom replied patiently. He didn't like any questions, but Vladimir had been a good employee for the few months Poolom had had him, and was a key man for the coming operation. "It will be big and far away. You will make a lot of money. I will make even more money. We'll get to kill some people. Not in Russia though, we're heading south. The items should arrive in three or four days. Make sure you know how to use them."

"Right," answered Vladimir. He knew all too well not to be too inquisitive. He'd personally seen Poolom kill an employee who had been caught stealing. Poolom and another of the pirates had beaten him with thick bamboo poles until the man looked like a pounded chicken breast, not a man. When he had found out that the man had been caught stealing a $50 watch from the loot from robbing the crew of a small tramp steamer, he decided that one, Poolom was a security obsessed psychopath, two, Vladimir would always be honest, three, he would get another job as soon as the opportunity presented itself. So far, his contacts with the Russian mafia hadn't found him anything yet, but he was biding his time and being careful. He had fifteen other Russians in the crew, the rest were a mixture of Africans, Indians, and Malays, but he only trusted (up to a point) the Russians. He made a point to never talk to them unless they were on one of their monthly "Let off steam" leaves into Jakarta, Surabaya, or Kuala Lumpur to drink, womanize, gamble and engage in other manly pirate pursuits.

Poolom knew that interest in his activities by law enforcement would pick up. While the Indonesians might temporarily be in chaos, the Americans, Japanese, Chinese, Indians, Australians, and other nations of the world would take an increased interest in preventing an expansion of piracy. This was another reason why it was a good move to expand outside of his usual sphere of activity and strike where no one would be expecting him. The strike on the Japanese whalers would leave most people wondering what had even happened. With the unpopularity of whaling, many would applaud the action, and with luck, the ice, cold, and bad weather might erase all traces of the theft. Investigators might perhaps guess that some fluke weather or storm had destroyed the Japanese whaling fleet. The Antarctic seas were particularly unforgiving and treacherous, especially with the icebergs present at this time of the year. He smiled at the prospect of more violence against the Japanese, a people he hated worse than any other.

Chapter 14

Acquisitions

"Every noble acquisition is attended with its risks; he who fears to encounter the one must not expect to obtain the other"-- Pietro Metastasio

Far away from Austin, Texas and the Antarctic, a submarine gets lost.

The Argentine navy submarine *Admiral Mendoza* is at dock at the submarine base of Mar del Plata. Captained by Arturo Lavigna, the Dolphin class diesel electric submarine was designed by Ingenieurkontor Lübeck Prof Gabler Nachf GmbH, a subsidiary of Howaldtswerke-Deutsche Werft AG (HDW) based in Lübeck, Germany and built by Thyssen Nordseewerke shipyards in Emden, Germany. Originally built for the State of Israel, she had been resold, in the ever-thrifty ways of navies to Argentina when Israel had upgraded their submarine fleet.

She was a formidable vessel. With a range of 8000 miles it had 10 forward torpedo tubes capable of launching the wire-guided Atlas Elektronik DM2A3 torpedoes carrying an almost 600 lb warhead or the surface to surface anti-ship missile the Harpoon. Its torpedo tubes could also be used for laying mines or for delivering divers for commando operations.

A later design upgrade of the original Dolphin, it featured an antimagnetic coating reducing the threat from magnetic mines and detection systems, and an Air Independent Propulsion system. The AIP was based on using a fuel cell to generate electric to run the electric propulsion system. It allowed the submarine to stay submerged for up to three weeks. With the inherently quiet operation of a diesel electric boat, it made the *Admiral Mendoza* very hard to detect in the water, even with the most modern sonar or magnetic detection technologies in the U.S. Navy.

Originally purchased with the idea of giving the Argentine navy an advantage in a future conflict to regain the Falkland Islands, that dream had faded with deepening economic problems and internal unrest which had turned military resources inward, and had left the *Admiral Mendoza* without a mission.

This left its captain with little to do. Captain Lavigna was a man with many debts, divorced, and an exception for South America, a man with no close family, born to a poor one. He had made few friends, and had advanced himself solely by his competence. Now in his fifties, he faced the prospect of a retirement that would be supplemented by a most inadequate pension. His career was his life, and he had learned every aspect of the ships systems as he felt was his duty. He found it hard to fill his days in port. His crew was reduced to a skeleton of housekeepers who kept the boat clean and seaworthy, but her days of voyaging beneath the seas seemed to be past. All the major subsystems were in good working order as befit something built with German craftsmanship and the diligence of the sparse crew.

Pietro Columbari was another man who remembered the better days of the Argentine Navy. Now in command of the Mar del Plata naval base and waiting for his retirement, he knew this was his last command he would ever have. Attending a society ball for a local charity, he was already tired from an evening of platitudes with prominent people who had little understanding for the navy. A graying, middle-aged man and an engineer by training, he had little ability for small talk. He had come to the navy through the wishes of his father, an old navy man, also an admiral. Now disillusioned, he had little loyalty left for a country that had left so many good navy men unemployed or underemployed.

A tall thin man clad in an elegantly tailored tuxedo approached the Admiral. He was extremely handsome and well tanned. "Admiral Columbari, I presume. The Flores' family wanted me to introduce myself to you. My name is Fabian Morelos from Peru."

One of his few close friends, the Flores brothers had connections in the maritime industries around the seaport and as such, Columbari had become a good acquaintance of the family.

"They regretted they could not be here tonight, but their business in North America went on longer than they had planned," continued Morelos.

Columbari took Fabian's hand and they began a polite conversation. The Admiral soon warmed to the young man. "He seems very knowledgeable of navy affairs," thought the Admiral, "I wish more Argentines had his knowledge."

Fabian turned the topic to the reason for the meeting, "I have heard of your unfortunate condition of your wife. You must accept my sincere wishes and prayers for a speedy recovery." This truly won the Admiral's heart. His wife was not from a navy or rich family. Although young, they had married for love. Because of his marriage, his superiors and other family members had ignored his plight. His wife was severely ill with a complex case of cancer. She needed superior medical attention than what was available in Argentina. Touched by the evident concern of the young man, he was unprepared for the next statement. Fabian continued on. "I wish I could help you in some way, Admiral. You are a good man, a good seaman, and you have been shabbily treated by your government."

Fabian Carlos Morelos was another of Bwana Doc's confederates. Well versed in the cultures of the various South American states, he moved seamlessly from one to the other, making a bribe here, setting up a business there, and always walking among the finest and richest of South American society. Tall and elegantly thin, versed in a thousand social skills, he carried himself like a sword ready to be stabbed at an unsuspecting victim. Bwana Doc had specifically told him to find the Admiral in charge of the submarine fleet at Mar del Plata. Mohammed Gamali knew that the Admiral was in desperate financial straits, and had made small items from naval stores available on the black market. He'd informed Bwana Doc of this—for a considerable amount of money.

Then Fabian threw the bait with a hook in it. "I've heard how you've been able to help Mohammed Gamali in matters of supply. He speaks most highly of you."

The Admiral's eyes bugged out sharply and his alarm at this disclosure almost caused him to spill his glass of Los Vascos.

"Who was this man?" he thought to himself. He had been supplying Gamali with certain marine stores for over a year. A generator here, a spare cannon barrel, missiles, even. Inventory at the naval base was never very good, and with so many ships laid up, supplies would not be missed for quite a while, if ever.

The Admiral was not a particularly venal or corrupt man. The neglect of the government for the navy coupled with his wife's illness, had pushed him over an edge which as in most South American countries was never very far from whatever plate you happened to be sitting on. Gamali had approached him over the matter of special tools for repairing the tracking systems on a type of marine radar. The slippery slope had been easy to slide over, and Columbari now had a dedicated account in Uruguay to facilitate payment. If this man intended blackmail, it could go badly for the Admiral. Argentine prisons were as bad as any in the world, and at best the Admiral might be forced to retire without a pension. His alarm grew as he considered the implications of Fabian's words.

Fabian continued on smoothly as if nothing had happened. "Do not be alarmed. Your dealings are completely confidential with me. In fact, I would like the opportunity to do you a favor and discuss these matters further with you at a more discreet time. I think I can offer you a mutually beneficial and lucrative arrangement that would address your needs. As we both know, long conversations lead to long ears."

The Admiral glanced around at the crowd in the large room. "Certainly you are correct. Could I suggest tomorrow at 13:00

hours at the Museo del Mar? I think you will find the shell exhibit most enjoyable, a remarkable collection by Benjamin Sisterna. Any man with as much knowledge of the sea as you have will be sure to enjoy it."

"Indeed, I have often heard of this collection. I will see you tomorrow," and Fabian Morelos took his leave.

The Admiral met him promptly at 1:00. The exhibit was not crowded as was usual during the week. The modern museum in the crowded downtown of Mar del Plata housed the 30,000 seashells that made up the outstanding collection. Fabian remarked upon its exceptional nature. "A life of dedication, Admiral, only a life of dedication can accomplish such a beautiful assemblage of shells. Remarkable."

"Or money," remarked the Admiral replied dryly.

"I'm so glad you brought that up, Admiral, and such a true statement. That brings me to the subject of our meeting. My associates and I would like to have you help us out with a certain naval activity. I believe your good friend Captain Lavigna also helps with Mr. Gamali's purchases."

The Admiral swallowed hard. Clearly they knew everything about their little theft operation. Lavigna had been particularly useful as he was one of the few captains of the ship that was frequently on base and had an intimate technical knowledge of the items requested, and where they were located. He had been a willing participant with his old friend who he knew needed the money as much as he did.

"He's a very good old shipmate. We've known each other for 30 years. We were in the Falklands war together."

I know, Admiral. Well, our needs are simple. We'd like Captain Lavigna to get orders to take his submarine, "Admiral Mendoza," out to sea on a training mission. And we'd like to hire him into our employment. Once that training mission is on its way, we will pay you the sum of $5,000,000, and once we've finished it, we'll pay Captain Lavigna the same amount.

The consequences of this training mission, however, will be considerable. You will have to leave Argentina. We will arrange that for you. Your wife needs medical treatment—we have already located one of the best oncologists in the world in the city of Baltimore in the United States, and they are ready to help you.

Columbari was astounded. All of his problems were solved. Catarina would live. His retirement was assured. His children's education was guaranteed.

"Just sailing orders? But what about the crew? They have mostly been reassigned or are on leave," he objected.

"We will supply the crew. You will need to issue orders to the guardhouse at the entrance to base. A special contingent of sailors will be arriving for training on the *Admiral Mendoza*. But we will need Captain Lavigna to command the submarine. No one knows its systems like he does. Your other job is to secure his help. After the payment and the mission, we will help him relocate anywhere he desires in the world, just as we will help you."

"I'll talk to him. I can't promise his cooperation."

"Admiral, I'm sure you can persuade him. You are old friends and there is no future for you in Argentina now. It is a sad thing to say, but the country has deserted its military heroes. They are treated like yesterday's newspaper."

The veiled threat was obvious in Fabian's silken words. Their thefts would be made known if they did not cooperate. He then explained exactly what he wanted Lavigna to do.

"You can contact me at this cell phone number once you have spoken to the good Captain.

One of Mar del Plata's humid spring days was coming to an end. Lavigna decided to take a walk into the city and have a few drinks before going home to his modest apartment. Seemingly by chance, he ran into his commanding officer, Admiral Columbari.

"Admiral, what a pleasure", the short thin captain exclaimed to his old friend, shaking his hand warmly. "Let's take a glass of wine together."

"Yes, lets, it has been too long. Come walk with me. I have something I need to discuss with you."

Settling in a quiet street side café, Columbari outlined the situation. While initially alarmed, Lavigna grew excited. "It's a way out at last. No miserable pension in a walk up apartment waiting to die. What do I have to do?"

"It's very easy, really" and Columbari explained the scheme.

During the week, a fueling truck pulled up to the *Admiral Mendoza*. It pumped a fresh supply of hydrogen into the storage tanks of the Siemens proton exchange membrane fuel cell. Another truck delivered liquid oxygen later in the week. Unfortunately, the diesel fuel lighter was down for repairs that week and so no more diesel fuel could be added to the submarine's tanks. The Admiral had of course ordered this refueling and the skeleton crew on board handled the limited amount of work that went into these necessary activities.

On the night of February 12th, a waning gibbous moon was high over the quiet sea base of Mar del Plata. *Suboficial Primero* Baldo Gomez was bored. It was a Saturday night and here he was stuck in useless guard duty with two other equally bored naval marines. The chief petty officer gave a long yawn and kicked his heels on the pavement in back of the gate sealing the base. Most of the seamen left on the base were in town, drinking and womanizing. He drew this duty once a month and always found it particularly tedious. There were no threats to the base to speak of, except the occasional attempts by thieves to break in. He felt like an underpaid night watchman.

A large military truck turned into the street leading up to gate. It decelerated slowly and came to a halt. A tall, thin naval lieutenant got out of the passenger's side.

The *Suboficial* came out to greet him. The lieutenant was crisply attired in a freshly pressed khaki uniform. The petty officer saluted him and the lieutenant saluted him back sharply. "Good evening, chief petty officer. Here are my orders and a gate pass."

Baldo opened the orders slowly. A special contingent of naval men had been ordered to training on the submarines of the naval base. They were to be allowed admittance and given to the care of Captain Lavigna.

Baldo knew Lavigna well, a decent stick, treated shabbily as they all had been. He had a lot of compañeros that had been laid off with shoddy pensions.

"Well, I'd be glad to help you out, *Tenente*. But we haven't received any orders here. We need a corresponding order from the base commander, Admiral Columbari, to let you through. It's a security rule. Stupid, I know, but the old man would have my hide."

"Tenente" Fabian Morelos eased his hand into his coat pocket. The powerful Taser multiple charge stun gun stood ready to incapacitate Gomez if he caused any problems. Yuraham Mitzna, the driver, likewise eased his hand onto the 9 mm Ruger automatic in his pocket.

"Subprimero Gomez, I forget to tell you," one of his command came up to him. "The Admiral's office sent these orders over before you came on duty." He handed Gomez a sheaf of papers.

"Ah ha," as he opened them and read their contents." "These confirm your orders, *Tenente*. My apologies. Enter and have a pleasant night. I'll call the guard at the pier for the *Admiral Mendoza* so you won't have any trouble with him."

The two men in the truck relaxed. They had planned to incapacitate the men at the gate, deliver the crew, and then make their way back out any way they could. The guard saluted Morelos again and beckoned to the man at the guardhouse back to open the gate.

The gray painted truck roared through, carrying the Israeli submarine crew in its back.

In a short time, the Israelis had disembarked on the pier where Lavigna met them personally. He had given the other members of the housekeeping crew the night's leave off. They were happy to go as there was nothing as bad as spending the night on a ship at harbor when there were warm beds and warmer women available in town.

Lavigna shook Morelos hand. "Good to meet you. I've taken the trouble of bringing up all the ship's systems to save time. We're ready to disconnect from land power."

Morelos' beckoned to Mitzna. "Lieutenant Mitzna is very familiar with this type of boat, if you could help get him and his men settled at appropriate stations that would speed things along."

"Request permission to come aboard, Captain," said Mitzna, standing to attention.

"Granted. Welcome Mr. Mitzna, to the *Admiral Mendoza*. Do you know these boats well?

"Yes, served in ones like her for 10 years in the Israeli navy," replied Mitzna.

"Well, then you should feel right at home," said Lavigna, impressed. He liked the well-set up young Israeli on sight, and they continued their discussion of submarines as they headed down into the ship. Inside, the entire length of the submarine could be seen from the conn deck. This was one of the unique traits of the Dolphin class subs; the relative openness of their layout. The crewmen settled down to the familiar workstations of the submarine, the engine room, the command and control area, and the torpedo rooms fore and aft.

Lavigna returned from his chores with the new crew to Morelos. "We have one problem. The guard on the pier and the guards at the other piers aren't expecting the "Admiral Mendoza" to leave tonight. They may create an alarm."

"I've been expecting that," said Fabian. "I'll take care of them. And don't worry about them, they won't be hurt, Bwana Doc doesn't like killing."

It was the first time Lavigna had heard that name. He wondered about it, but he had much to do to get the submarine and the new crew ready for sea.

Fabian left the submarine and returned to the truck. He got back in the truck, this time in the driver's seat, started and turned it around and stopped by the guard farther down the dock. The guard looked up at the unusual sight of a *Tenente* driving a truck.

"It's a pleasant night, *Marinero Primero*, how would you like a bottle to keep you company?"

Able Seaman Juan Davila knew he shouldn't have anything to drink on duty, but it was difficult to refuse an officer.

"No sir! Anything would be most welcome, sir!" he exclaimed, saluting briskly.

Morelos reached down into the duffel bag by the gear ship and hauled out a bottle of Argentine "Whiskey Ramsay." The seaman's eyes widened as he took the bottle. It would be a good night and a lot less tedious than he had been expecting.

Morelos dispensed several more bottles to guards along the way and finished off with the good *Suboficial Primero* and his two men at the gate. He roared off into the night. He knew the guards would sleep well tonight as all the bottles had been liberally laced with a powerful tasteless sedative. A minimum number of eyes would watch the *Admiral Mendoza* depart.

The *Admiral Mendoza* slipped quietly out of the naval base of Mar del Plata in the early morning hours. The harbor of the naval base was brightly lit with sodium vapor lights, but Lavigna knew the way out of the harbor like he knew the inside of a bathtub and could have found his way out if it were pitch black. Few people were about and even fewer paid attention. The harbormaster watch duly noted that Admiral Columbari had issued sailing orders for the submarine. As their usual watch was at night, they had no notice of the apparent lack of preparation for the sailing. The guards were sufficiently groggy and gave no alarm. They would remember less the next day. No ships came and went. Some fishermen remarked it was unusual for a submarine to leave at this time of the night, but nothing came of the desultory comments. Lavigna guided the boat out through the harbor navigation lights himself. The guard boat for the base gave them no hail as it was far on the other side of the harbor when they came through. Once beyond sight of the shore,

Lavigna had the vessel submerge and he set the course he had been given by the admiral. By dawn, he was out of sight from any prying eyes either on or above the oceans. He was to reach the rendezvous point and then wait for the arrival of a certain ship. At this point he would be well beyond Argentine waters and far from observation.

In the waning light of the next day, Bwana Doc and Wan Fu stood on the bridge of the converted oil well drilling ship, *Alistair Billings*. The ship was a camouflaged wonder. Originally intended for drilling oil wells in relatively shallow waters, she had become obsolete through the frequent advances in drilling technology that took place in the world's persistent search for new oil supplies. Bwana Doc had picked her up for a song at a yard where she had been destined to be sold for scrap. He had sent her to a shipyard in Poland for an involved refit. The large derrick on top had been removed and the space now covered with hatches, she now looked from the surface like a simple cargo freighter. Beneath the hatches however, she had an enormous moon pool equipped with a variety of high capacity cranes and davits. The ship had also been refitted with an elaborate electronics suite including state of the art radar and sonar. To complete her rebirth, she had been given engines that could make her go twice as fast as the typical cargo freighter.

Bwana Doc and the enormous Asian scanned the horizon with their powerful 20 X 80 Steiner binoculars for the *Admiral Mendoza*. They knew that their radar would immediately detect the periscope as it came up to check for the rendezvous. The captain of the ship, a burly Scotsman named Willy Roberson, also scanned the horizon.

"Maybe that Argentine swab just took our money and ran," growled the Scotsman with a slight burr.

"I do not think so—Fabian says he is like the Admiral with his own particular ethical dilemma and, like the Admiral, he had little to hold him in Argentina and needs employment," said Wan Fu in his precise manner. "In any case, our crew is onboard the boat now and Mr. Mitzna has his orders if Captain Lavigna deviates from the planned rendezvous.

"We have a sound signature consistent with a boat of the *Admiral Mendoza*'s type. Bearing 275 degrees" announced the sonar operator.

"Periscope signal off the starboard bow, same bearing. About 4 kilometers away." sang out the radioman. "She's headed this way."

The group focused on the horizon and waited.

"Ah, see, there is the periscope, now, I see it," said Bwana Doc. "Willy, begin sending the blinker signal now and wait for his response. Tell the crews in the moon pool to make ready. Sonar locators on and scanning. I want an exact position on the submarine at all times. But wait with the flood lights and underwater cameras until he's closer."

Lavigna and Mitzna saw the big cargo ship on the horizon through the monitor hooked to the periscope camera. Easily four times the length of the *Admiral Mendoza* they knew they had the right ship from the description given to Columbari by Morelos.

"Let's head her in, Yuraham," ordered Lavigna, "we've got a rendezvous to make."

Directed by Robertson, the signalman on the bridge began a rapid series of dot and dash flashes, instructing the submarine. Radio silence was being observed. Although they suspected no pursuit, no chances were to be taken. The submarine came nearer and nearer and turned parallel to the *Alistair Billings*. Coming to within 50 meters, and matching speeds with the ship, she began to submerge.

"15 meters depth at the sail", Captain," the sonarman on the bridge announced.

"She's cut her engines."

"All power off!" Have the dive team standing by!" barked Robertson. "Once we're dead in the water, engage starboard side thrusters and bring us over her." The large turbine thrusters on the ship whirred to life. Designed to keep the ship precisely positioned for drilling operations, they moved the massive ship like a ballet dancer pirouetting across a dance floor. "Turn on the floodlights in the moon pool and the remote cameras. Bring us to where she sits precisely over the moon pool."

When refitted and the derrick removed, the moon pool that allowed the drill equipment to access the seafloor had been greatly enlarged. Now covered by the hatches of the ship and darkness, the transfer would be totally discreet from the prying eyes of satellites and stray vessels that might come into range. "In position, Captain." announced the helmsman. The positional display showed the submarine squarely in the middle of the large ship, but well below where her keel would have been. "Three pings with the sonar, let her come up." Ping, ping, ping and the submarine began to rise on the monitor.

Lavigna and Mitzna slowly released ballast seawater from the ship. They inched the ship up toward the large brightly lit opening, which they could not see and they had to trust the unknown crew of the *Billings*. Both men had strained faces and sweaty hands as the ship rose slowly meter-by-meter into the light.

"Divers back from the edge of the moon pool. No matter how slowly he brings her up, there's still going to be a splash. But be ready with the mooring lines," boomed Roberson into the public address system of the moon pool deck. The group of twenty divers complied, stepping well back from the edge of what looked like an enormous swimming pool.

The large gray bulbous submarine surfaced like a steel whale under the floodlights of the moon pool. Roberson gave orders to flood the ballast on the *Alistair Billing*, making her sink deeper in the water and bringing the *Admiral Mendoza* higher up in the moon pool. The divers jumped in and secured the ship with stout hawsers as best they could. Davits lowered cables that would be slung under the ship, connected and then tightened, securing her from any storms. Stout chains augmented the securing process. The Billings would look as though she was carrying a good size cargo, which indeed she was. When the *Admiral Mendoza* was high enough, the moon pool doors were closed. Now when viewed from the bottom or the top, the ship would look like a slightly unusual cargo ship. There was no trace of the submarine to any prying surveillance satellites.

Gangways were laid to the submarine. Bwana Doc and Wan Fu greeted Captain Lavigna and the rest of the crew. Understandably nervous at first, they soon warmed to a couple of shots of Monopolowa vodka. One of Roberson's officers showed the crew to their quarters where they soon were in their bunks for a well-earned rest. Their training for the mission would begin tomorrow. Bwana Doc related the transfer of the money to Lavigna's account and allowed him to check that it had occurred using a ship's laptop with a satellite internet link. Lavigna nodded with satisfaction. The Admiral had not steered him wrong.

"But what of Admiral Columbari? What will be done about him?" asked Lavigna, concerned for his old friend that had allowed him to acquire this bounty.

"Your friend and his family are safely in the United States by now and Catherina has already been examined by top oncologists," reported Bwana Doc cheerfully. "Her prognosis is bright. Your friend sends you his best wishes. As far as the Argentine government, there is no record of him leaving Mar de Plata and his car is about to be involved in a serious fiery accident, which the newspapers will believe, was the act of terrorists. Investigators will find four bodies, a man and woman and two children that will match the bodies of the Admiral and his family. These are bodies taken from the Buenos Aires morgue. Fabian Morelos is most resourceful. While they won't survive a detailed forensic examination, they don't have to; they just have to buy us a few weeks time."

"But what do you really want from me? Who are you?"

"I am Bwana Doc and you are going to help me right some great wrongs in the world, if you want. If you don't, that's fine. We will put you on the first plane we can with the payment agreed upon, and you can go and live a life of luxury. Or you can help run this submarine and do some good in the world, and make even more money. It's up to you."

"I'm a seaman, first and foremost—I like the crew you picked— good men and I think they like me. If it involves the sea, I'm game. I was born and bred a sailor. I know a lot about being treated wrongly, too," He added stoutly.

"Good. We need skilled men of determination. We'll talk more of it tomorrow. Rest now, it's been a stressful time,' as he led Lavigna back to his quarters. He issued orders to Captain Roberson to obtain certain items from the *Admiral Mendoza* and deliver them to one of the Zodiacs while the final securing of the submarine was taking place in the vast hold.

Submarine secured, the *Alistair Billings* set sail away from the Argentine coast. Equipped with powerful engines that let her make twice the speed of an ordinary cargo ship, she headed south. By dawn she was well behind the Falkland Islands where no Argentine aircraft would go. Driving south during the day, she began to encounter her first ice floes from the melting Antarctic ice cap.

D. R. Schneider

Then they sailed east, giving the Falklands and Sandwich islands a wide berth. They did not want to attract the attention of Royal Navy air reconnaissance or radar. While it was hoped that complete security had been achieved in the submarine kidnap, it would be well to be as far way from Argentine waters and the Argentine air force as possible. They would lose themselves in the trackless Southern Ocean as they headed for another rendezvous.

Chapter 15

People get upset when their submarines go missing

"Every gun that is made, every warship launched, every rocket fired, signifies in the final sense a theft from those who hunger and are not fed, those who are cold and are not clothed". --Dwight D. Eisenhower

Meanwhile, back in Mar del Plata, the sailing of the *Admiral Mendoza* had not gone unnoticed. A boat that had not sailed in months does not normally sail without some preparation and notification. The crew had been unaware the boat was leaving. The delivery of the hydrogen and oxygen had been noted during the week prior to sailing. While a brief cruise was sometimes scheduled to check out systems on the boat and these were generally left to the discretion of the commander upon his admiral's approval, these were always only overnight trips close inshore. On such a cruise, a couple of dives might take place and the submarine might run for several hours underwater to test the underwater propulsion systems. Other than that the submarine would be in continuous contact with shore based radio command headquarters. The radio silence of the submarine was unremarked upon by noon of the next day of its departure, remarked upon by the early afternoon, and a subject of serious discussion by the nightfall that came late at this time of the year. Admiral Guillermo Ferrari, Columbari's second in command was unable to reach his superior. By that time of course, the submarine was deep in the belly of the

117

D. R. Schneider

Alistair Billings. Shore and ship based radar sweeps revealed nothing resembling a submarine on the surface. He initiated a general alarm and reported the facts of the matter as far as they were known to his superiors. Alarm grew general throughout the night. By dawn of the next day, a search was begun. Repeated sweeps by Grumman G-2 Tracker patrol planes revealed nothing, not even radar echoes resembling a periscope. By midday, a general alert was issued. By the afternoon, a slick of diesel fuel and a debris field were found floating on the surface about 100 miles out from Mar del Plata. Inspection by seaplane helicopters and patrol craft reveals insulation, clothes, and other items consistent with material from the *Admiral Mendoza*. This had, of course, been the items taken from the submarine by Captain Roberson. Ships sounded the bottom searching for the sonar profile of the wreck, but nothing was found. Admiral Guillermo Ferrari's concern and worry now turned to suspicion. Although a submarine can sink and debris be found, the area was too shallow to have broken the submarine's pressure hull that would have brought such debris to the surface. Repeated magnetometer sweeps had only found already charted wrecks. Sweeps upstream from the debris field also came up negative. Nor was there any sign of a rescue buoy from the submarine indicating that whatever had happened had not involved any type of warning or perceived threat. Ferrari requested permission to call in the United States Navy to aid in the search. Given the rampant nationalism present in the Argentine Navy, this was a step of epic proportions. Losing a submarine

118

could not be kept secret, however, and soon the newspapers, television stations and Internet were reporting the story. Pressure from the media finally resulted in the U.S. Navy being consulted. The detection of submarine wrecks was never an easy task even though the area was fairly defined and shallow. A United States National Oceanographic and Atmospheric Administration (NOAA) survey vessel specializing in deep underwater research as well a U.S. Navy frigate with advanced antisubmarine and search capabilities sailed down from the Caribbean and were there in a week. Although hope of recovery of the submarine's crew had faded, an answer was needed. The submarine had cost the Argentine government $200,000,000 and questions needed to be answered. Repeated searching by the Americans revealed no wreckage resembling the submarine.

By now the mystery and uproar was general. The apparent death of Columbari and his family in the explosion of his car had only served to fuel speculation on what had happened and had lead people to believe terrorists had kidnapped Columbari, forced him to issue the fueling and sailing orders and then stolen the submarine. But there was no word from any of the usual organizations. No one claimed responsibility. It all seemed too strange. The delayed forensic analysis revealed that the bodies in the car were not Columbari and his family was the first break in the investigation. This turned the investigation back to the Admiral who was nowhere to be found. None of his few relatives had any ideas either where the Admiral and his family were.

D. R. Schneider

The answer came from an expatriate Argentine who was having a night on the town in Rio de Janeiro. Raul Romero had come to Rio for a good time and was having it. Hanging out in a bar on Ipanema Beach, he had not yet decided which one of the local women he was going to spend his evening when he heard a man speaking Spanish in the characteristic rapid fire Argentine dialect. Glad to see a fellow countryman, he greeted with a friendly, "*Che, pebe como vai*"? Already considerably drunk, the thin man with the erect bearing greeted him equally warmly. After a few more drinks, talk inevitably turned to the story of the day, the disappearance of the submarine. The man revealed that he was actually a former Argentine sailor who had served with Columbari. He related that he had seen the strangest thing at the airport in Rio. He had flown into Rio on his company's private jet and the jet next to his was being refueled. The passengers had gotten out to stretch their legs. They were a man, a woman and two young children. He swore that the man was Columbari. Even though he now lived in Venezuela and it had been many years since he had been in the navy he was sure. The next day, the other man contacted the Argentine embassy. Further questioning by the Argentine military attaché and showing the man a picture of Columbari and his family confirmed the man's conviction that he had seen the Admiral the day the submarine supposedly sailed. Efforts to locate the plane came to a dead end. Her identification numbers were taken from a plane that had crashed two months earlier in China. It had filed a flight plan for Rabat, Morocco but no evidence could be found it had ever reached there. An alert went out throughout the world. A submarine had been stolen and pirates or terrorists may have taken it.

In reality the flight had flown to a small private airstrip in northern Brazil where a second jet took the family on to the Bahamas where they were given new Mexican passports to the United States. With assumed names, the Columbari family went on to visit the clinic in the United States found by Bwana Doc's people and Catherina's new cancer treatment was begun.

The first thought in Interpol was that Columbian drug dealers had taken the submarine. The Columbian drug cartel had tried for years to build submarines that could be used in drug smuggling. They had even built one in the Andes Mountains that was going to be brought down to the coast for operation. The submarine builders of the world were well aware by now of their desires and carefully screened any prospective buyers. With vast amounts of money at their disposal, it always remained a possible threat.

Bennett Boyd had been kept informed of the status of the search as soon as the disappearance of Columbari had come to the notice of the authorities.

"Assuming it's not the Columbians, who in the world needs to have a submarine?" she asked her staff.

Rudolf Delius, her precise, hardworking German second in command answered first. "This is not just any submarine. It is an almost state of the art submarine made for war. The Argentines may have not had the money to operate it, but this submarine will be hard to detect by any navy in the world, including the Americans."

"Why is that?" queried Boyd who knew a lot about the naval matters, but had never served in the submarines.

"For one thing, it has AIP, Air Independent Propulsion. For some reason, the German government let this be exported to Argentina with the submarine. It uses fuel cells to generate electricity for propulsion. It's very quiet, quieter than a nuclear submarine. It can stay underwater at least 3 weeks. It has an anechoic coating that absorbs sonar signals making location difficult. It is also constructed from nonmagnetic materials making magnetometer detection difficult. Its sail, the part above the hull incorporates stealth technology. Her radar signature will be very small. It was designed to go close in shore and can operate in as little as 20 meters of water. This submarine can be very hard to find if it doesn't want to be found.

"So we are talking about a sophisticated stealth warship, heavily armed."

"Yes, useful for smugglers, but it has a lot of other uses as well."

"Like piracy?" asked Bennett.

Rudolf nodded his red bearded head slowly up and down. "Yes, this ship could threaten any ship up to the size of a cruiser. It can sink any merchant ship afloat." It's relatively fast as well. It can catch any common merchant ship at cruising speed.

"Why did the Argentines need a vessel like that? The country is a basket case economically. I saw on a news broadcast where they had massive starvation on the streets of Buenos Aires."

Rudolf shrugged, "It's the same all over the world. African countries have submarines, jet aircraft and battleships with no food on the table for their people. There's nothing we can do about that. But we should be able to find this submarine, if it's not sunk. It needs logistical support to keep operating. It has to surface sometime and it can be seen by satellite."

"Send out bulletins to every port authority that might be able to service this submarine. You can never tell, there are eyes everywhere. But who ever did this is good at turning the good eye blind," said Bennett with finality. "We've got our work cut out for us—if it's terrorists we should hear something soon, but with pirates who knows?"

D. R. Schneider

Chapter 16

Whales

"The Cetacea hold an important lesson for us. The lesson is not about whales and dolphins, but about ourselves. There is at least moderately convincing evidence that there is another class of intelligent beings on Earth beside ourselves. They have behaved benignly and in many cases affectionately towards us. We have systematically slaughtered them. Little reverence for life is evident in the whaling industry - underscoring a deep human failing...In warfare, man against man, it is common for each side to dehumanize the other so that there will be none of the natural misgivings that a human being has at slaughtering another..." Carl Sagan

"Every one of these vanished millions of whales used to consume several hundred tons of a large species of zooplankton a year. That plankton now is undergoing a classic population explosion for want of a predator. What will be the effect on the oxygen-producing smaller plankton of the world ocean? What will be the effect on the colour and reflectivity of the oceans? What will be the effect on the average water temperature of the oceans, on its dissolved oxygen content and subsequently on the earth's atmosphere? No one knows. But climatologists know any significant change in ocean temperature can have profound effects on the earth's climates. By killing off the whales of the world man is playing Russian roulette with the earth's primary support system. Yes, we desperately need the whales to preserve the air we breathe."--George Small, Ph.D.

The pods of Minke whales continue their foraging for their main food, krill. Krill are small shrimp-like crustaceans less than ½ of an inch in length that form the keystone of much of the food web of the ocean. A vast resource, the Antarctic krill population alone is estimated at 500 million tons, more than the weight of humans on the globe. These crustaceans feed on the plants of the ocean, the phytoplankton that produce oxygen from seawater. Since a whale requires a lot of krill because of its size, feeding is a major part of the Minke's life. Surface feeding is done at night and day feeding is much deeper, always following the schools of krill as they migrate up and down through the ocean. Multiplying and growing with prodigal abundance in the Antarctic summer, the krill were captured by the Minke inhaling vast quantities of water containing the krill and then forcing the water out through baleen plates, specialized structures anchored in the gums of the whale's mouth. In the Minke they are about 6 inches in length. In the larger baleen whales like the fin and the blue whales, these plates can be up to three feet in length. Made of keratin, a structural protein, they filtered out the krill and allowed the captured seawater to be expelled back to the ocean. Baleen was another product from hunted whales—it was made into women's corsets and the ribs of umbrellas and parasols.

There are other whales in the oceans that whalers also hunt. Sperm whales, the largest predators of the ocean, are also on the list of whales to be killed in the name of research by the men of the *Yoshino Maru*. The whale made famous in the novel Moby Dick, sperm whales are found throughout the world and are also known as cachalot. Sperm whales have enormous heads with teeth instead of baleen. The males use the teeth in battles for dominance in herds. Sperm whales hunt the giant squid of the ocean depths in dives down to up to 10000 feet. In epic underwater battles during dives up to an hour, they feed on these huge cephalopods that are up to 40 feet in length. Scars from these encounters can often be seen on individuals, indicating that it is not a one-way contest. In the eternal dark of the deep ocean, the sperm whales find the squid in the same manner that bats find moths and other flying insects, through echolocation. Emitting a series of loud clicks that increase in frequency as they descend, the return signals allow them to build a three-dimensional picture of where their prey is. At the time of capture, the clicks are so frequent that they sound like a loud buzz.

Baleen whales also make sounds, but not apparently for echolocation. The most famous of these are, of course, the songs of the humpback whale. The purpose of these is much less clear. They may function in mating or be some complex means of communication. The song of the blue whale is the loudest sound made by any animal, and it may be heard halfway around the world, as sound travels better underwater than it does in air.

Sperm whales are producers of two unique substances, spermaceti and ambergris. The former is found in a large case in the head of the whale and is a white oily wax resembling semen (hence the name of the whale). This case may play a role in the echolocation system used in hunting. After killing, the whale's head would be opened and the spermaceti would be bailed out of the head of the whale with a bucket. Up to three tons of spermaceti could be obtained from a large male. Formerly used as a high quality ingredient in candles, ointments and cosmetics, it is now rarely obtainable and had been replaced commercially by jojoba oil. The other unique substance is ambergris, the intestinal secretion used in perfume manufacture. The indigestible beaks of the squid it uses as food may irritate the intestines of the whale and stimulate the production of ambergris. Sperm whales live in tightly knit groups consisting of a several females and their young. The females communally care for the young. Bull males only occasionally visit these groups. The selective harvesting of the largest sperm whales (males) has resulted in an overall decline in the size of the population and the size of the whales. At one time over a million sperm whales roamed the oceans of the world. Now only 350,000 were left.

How intelligent are whales? The problem in answering this question lies in the difficulty of defining intelligence. In the environment that whales live in, much of the skills that humans have are useless, therefore the intelligence to use these skills is not required. In the simplest and crudest measurements of intelligence, the weight of the brain compared to the weight of the body, whales and dolphins compare favorably with chimpanzees and humans. Their brain's anatomy is similar to that of man, albeit with much larger areas devoted to sound and its processing. The absolute brain size of the bottle-nosed dolphin is slightly larger than a human's and the brain of the sperm whale is the largest of any animal that has ever lived. The problem that we have in determining their intelligence is the completely alien nature of their environment. It is as difficult to imagine the intelligence required to live in a featureless buoyant environment where navigation is in three dimensions. Experiments done to determine the intelligence of dolphins and killer whales have given ambiguous results and much more needs to be done. It can be stated with some certainty that whales are at least as intelligent as an elephant and probably as intelligent as a chimpanzee. This would seem to place them in the same ethical framework as the higher apes, which are usually not used for food.

D. R. Schneider

Chapter 17

Visiting the Committee for Cetacean Research
Tokyo, Japan

"The saddest aspect of life right now is that science gathers knowledge faster than society gathers wisdom."--Isaac Asimov

"Ethics and Science need to shake hands."--Richard Clarke Cabot

Chevillac had had no trouble making an appointment with the Director General of the Committee for Cetacean Research. Describing herself as a chemist interested in the commercial aspects of whales immediately gave her credibility with the Japanese executive. Too few people, he felt, were interested in exploiting the whale resource. Too many of his visitors were misguided environmentalists who wanted him to stop "scientific whaling". And that his visitor was an exotic, still beautiful woman from Paris, France made him even more receptive to meeting her. Paris was his favorite city to visit and he enjoyed the open, non-judgmental nature of the French people to the habits and behavior of the Japanese. They were nicer than the rigid Americans that had banned all whale products from their country so many years ago. And, it was a wonderful opportunity to practice his French. He had taken lessons for years.

Madame Chevillac got down to business immediately. Smoking a Shepherd's Hotel cigarette in a holder, she studied the director

131

from beneath her carefully coiffed hair. Her company needed ambergris of a certain nature. Fresh from a whale—could he help?

The Director General spread his hands in despair. Little ambergris was collected at sea these days. Beachcombers found most of it on the shore. He would like to help the good lady but this was a complex request.

"You do not perhaps fully comprehend our need," she replied, finding the man's French atrocious, and difficult to understand. "We are willing to pay well for this ambergris, well above the market. But it must be fresh, cut from the belly of whale. Your institute kills whales, do they not?"

"Of course, we kill whales for scientific study," the director replied evenly. "But not for commercial purposes."

"But you sell the meat of the whales; you kill, do you not?" she countered.

"Well, of course, we have to cover our costs." His eyes blinking rapidly as he replied.

"Then you could kill a whale for me, couldn't you? No one would stop you," she said, batting her eyes and crossing her legs.

"You don't understand, Madame. Not all whales have ambergris, only sperm whales have it, and not all of them have it. Only a very few specimens do."

Chevillac knew the facts of ambergris production very well. "So, perhaps only one in twenty has this precious substance. There are twenty whales out there your ship could kill, no?"

"Yes, but, we have a research program. It cannot be interrupted."

"But sir, you have a mandate to conduct research on whales do you not? As well as maintain your funding, so that more good research can be conducted. No one would know except your people, would they? I have heard the Oceanwarriors fleet has been held up by engine trouble."

"Yes, it's true. Our fleet is not beleaguered by those pirates. Even the Australians have gone home." The director nodded in agreement. He knew that whale meat sales were not going well despite years of government campaigns. The cosmopolitan sensibilities of a new generation of Japanese attuned to the opinions of the world, and a taste for imported beef and lamb, had reduced whale meat sales dramatically. His backers now had large amounts of whale meat in freezers and were trying to export it to China, Russia, and other Asian markets. Additional backing would indeed be helpful from any source.

"And our need is an urgent one. We need the ambergris as soon as possible or our research program will be interrupted."

"As you know our fleet is at sea now and there are plenty of sperm whales in the vicinity," answered the director. "It might be possible to enlarge the scope of our research to cover sperm whales."

"*D'accord!* I knew you were a reasonable man the moment I heard your excellent French!" exclaimed Madame Chevillac.

D. R. Schneider

In the end, the arrangement was made. A €20,000,000 donation would be made to the Committee "for research". A two million Euro deposit would be sent to a Swiss account to be set up for the director. Instructions for shipping the ambergris were given to the director. Chevillac left, well satisfied, she had the best whale hunters in the world looking for the substance that would make her wealthier than she had ever dreamed possible. A few whales would die for it, but as the Americans say, you can't make an omelet without breaking a few eggs.

Chapter 18

Hiding a Submarine
(is harder than hiding a whale)

"Hiding places there are innumerable, escape is only one, but possibilities of escape, again, are as many as hiding places."--Franz Kafka

"One of life's primal situations; the game of hide and seek. Oh, the delicious thrill of hiding while the others come looking for you, the delicious terror of being discovered, but what panic when, after a long search, the others abandon you! You mustn't hide too well. You mustn't be too good at the game. The player must never be bigger than the game itself." -- Jean Baudrillard

Olaf Arviddson was completing his count of snowy sheathbills when he stopped to watch an albatross heading out to sea. It was a frosty day, like all the days on Bouvet Island, but not as cold as it would be. The squat shape of the volcanic top of the island was hidden in clouds as it frequently was. The wind seemed to bluster all the time, a great deal like his home in the Lofoten Islands in Norway, although this was more desolate. Arviddson had an affinity for the barren island. Bouvet Island, or Bouvetøya, as the Norwegians called it, was the world's most remote island. Four miles long, it was 1,000 miles from Antarctica. A volcanic land, it was covered mostly by glaciers and completely uninhabited— except for birds and seals. It had no harbors or ports and only has an unmanned weather station.

A tall, blond man, clad in bright yellow heavy weather gear, Arviddson was starkly visible against the black volcanic sand of the beach. A video record taken by a camera mounted on his head was supplementing his manual counting. Outlandishly attired as he was, it was functional, and his documentation of the nesting population was complete. The group had come five days ago from the Troll Antarctic Station in Queen Maude Land far to the south. The Norwegian station was the only one in this part of Antarctica, and visits to Bouvet were irregular at best. The other team members were not far away, completing the counting of seals and other sea birds. Other members were refitting the automated weather station and anchoring it against the horrendous storms that swept the island. A ship carrying a helicopter to ferry them back to the Troll Antarctic Station was expected to pick them up tomorrow.

He was watching the albatross as it flew out to sea when suddenly the clouds banking around the island opened up. Much to his surprise, he saw two ships close together. They were so close that he could see people moving around on the decks. Unaware that his video camera was recording the two ships, he stood watching them for several minutes until the clouds swirled over the strange apparition and they vanished as if they had never been there.

Far from the shipping lanes, in a deserted stretch of ocean within sight of Bouvet Island in the deep South Atlantic, the *Alistair Billings* met the tanker *Walter Wilt*. The tanker, a member of Bwana Doc's global fleet of ships that were at his disposal, was needed to complete the fueling of the submarine. It had only partially fueled with diesel by the Argentine navy, a fact only discovered after the submarine had been acquired. The *Billings* could not fuel the submarine from her own tanks as she was a fuel oil powered vessel. Luckily, the *Walter Wilt* was in port in India and was not that far away from the *Alistair Billings*. Fueling the boat was speedily accomplished and the *Alistair Billings* was soon on its way toward to the south of the Cape of Good Hope. Far to the south, they sailed into the blowing bad weather one could only find in the Southern Ocean. Attentive to their tasks and eager to get underway, no one on board noticed the man in the brightly colored gear standing on the black volcanic beach highlighted against the glaciers that covered most of the island.

Secure in the warm cabins of the *Billings*, the crew of the newly renamed *Retter der Wale* (Savior of the Whales) trained for the coming task aboard the tenable submarine as well as they could with a submarine that had been secured from the ocean. They were promised ample sea time to complete their training once they were closer to their goal. They were excited about their mission. To actually use a ship's weapons on something was always exciting, and Bwana Doc had promised them all that no one would be killed unless it might happen to be in self-defense. This did not worry the crew. They were naval men, bred to a hard life of war, and many had been in combat like Lavigna and Mitzna.

They were being extremely well paid, with good quarters, and were being treated with respect—what more could a man want? If they were supposed to sink a ship or two--well, they had been prepared to do that for many a year, and had been treated poorly and paid worse in that expectation when in the service. Already experienced in similar submarines, they were soon comfortable with taking the ship to sea once they had weathered the rough South Atlantic and arrived at their destination. While they trained on the suspended submarine, the crewmen of the *Alistair Billings* painted her entire hull a blinding white. This would further aid in camouflaging the submarine in the ice floes of the Antarctic and no one would be expecting a white submarine. All were uniformly gray or black.

They drove steadily eastwards toward their next rendezvous, oblivious to their sighting by the Norwegians.

Arviddson dutifully reported the sighting to his team leader, who in turn reported it to the commander of the research station. The commander had just received the Interpol bulletin about the loss of the submarine and the search for information of the Alistair Billings. Taking Arviddson's video, he had one of the computer people at the station enhance the imaging on the ship. He was able to see both the names of both of the vessels. Bennett Boyd's staff had been their usual thorough selves in notifying everyone they could think of about the unusual freighter. The commander immediately emailed her office about the sighting.

Bennett Boyd could only feel even more strongly that the *Alistair Billings* was somehow involved with the disappearance of the submarine, but proof was a long ways away. The presence of the *Walter Wilt* was a further conundrum. Records showed it listed as a "General Cargo Tanker", but the ownership was as difficult to determine as the *Alistair Billings* had been. This to her was equally suspicious. As her resources and time were limited in following through on what was really only a hunch on her part, she contented herself to keeping the available satellite surveillance looking for vessel's resembling the *Alistair Billings*. She put out a call to all naval forces in the area to provide any assistance they could in finding of the *Alistair Billings*.

The *Billings* arrived at its next rendezvous. Not far from the Crozet Islands, two fishing trawlers appeared on the horizon. Coming down from the port of Durban in South Africa, they were minimally crewed by some of Roberson's men and they were the next phase of training. In route, they had installed primitive, remote steering systems for the ships. The crews were evacuated by Zodiac and brought to the *Billings*.

The next day, the *Retter der Wale* was crewed, lowered back into the water and allowed to submerge. The two fish ships were moving in front of the track of the submarine. The *Billings* stayed well away from the practice sessions. The seas were rough and the wind was strong. It was just as Bwana Doc wanted. It could be that the weather would be good for the final phase but they could not count on it. It was always best to practice in bad weather.

Captain Lavigna was excited. He had only fired practice torpedoes a few times before and Mitzna was also eagerly anticipating the use of their weapons. Lavigna brought the crew to stations and the sonarman marked off the range of the target. The sophisticated ISUS 90-1 Total Control System or TCS of the submarine had already set the firing parameters within seconds after

139

sonar had acquired the target. Lavigna gave the order. The *Retter* fired one of her DMA2A4 torpedoes.

Running free and clear, her fiber optic cable spooled out behind and the TCS vectored her into the side of the tramp steamer where she exploded with a most satisfying roar. A pillar of smoke climbed to the horizon. As the smoke cleared, it was apparent the explosion of the 250-kilogram warhead had blown the ship in half. The two halves of the ship bobbed on the surface and then sank beneath the waves within minutes. The Captain played the entire attack on the submarine video and the crew responded with a hearty cheer as the torpedo went off. With a spectacular roar, the first of the tramp steamers blew up and sank almost immediately. Now it was time for the second vessel and the testing of the IDAS (Interactive Defense and Attack System). A short-range missile, it was fired directly from the torpedo tube and could also be used against aircraft and coastal targets. Also fiber optic cable guided, she was resistant to electronic counter measures just like the torpedo. Carried four to a tube, she carried an infrared camera allowing her to be steered to her target.

"IDAS ready" Yitzhak Canaan, the firing control officer announced. "Fire when ready," replied Lavigna. The missile was fired out of the torpedo tube by compressed air. As its solid fuel rocket motor ignited, it climbed into the frigid polar air. Buffeted by the strong wind, it was hard to control, but after a few jumps up and down, Yitzhak guided the missile smoothly into the bridge of the ship, producing a very satisfactory explosion. A small fire began to burn. The much smaller warhead of the missile made it harder for her to sink ships.

"A good hit, sir!" cried Canaan.

"Good work! Periscope depth please, Lieutenant!" responded Lavigna.

The periscope cameras revealed a nice fire on the ship, but no sign of sinking. "Shoot another, Mr. Canaan. Try to hit her in the stern."

Another missile away. With skillful accuracy, Canaan brought the missile in a little on the port side about 20 feet from the stern. Another explosion.

"A call from the *Alistair Billings*, sir! Aircraft on radar—approximately 100 miles away, way at 30,000 feet," cried Mitzna.

Bwana Doc reacted instantly. "End the exercise, Captain, submerge immediately. No periscope above water. Willy, have the *Billings* to resume course, full speed—you can follow by her acoustic signature."

Within minutes, the submarine was safely deep beneath the rough weather of the surface. The *Billings* was already steaming out of sight and the submarine followed her. The two ships made their way away from the burning ship with rapid speed. On the bridge of the *Retter,* Bwana Doc muttered some thoughts about how the world was getting too crowded for comfort, but he was content with how the mission was going. The training session had been necessary, and now he could be sure that they were ready for the next phase of the operation. Within an hour, the ship and its plume of smoke was well below the horizon.

The presence of the plane was an unusual event in these desolate realms, hence Bwana Doc's additional caution. While they knew that there was a small scientific research station on Crozet, there was no airfield as far as they were aware. Likewise, the Kerguellen Islands, their next nearest landfall had no aircraft stationed there.

If they had known, they would have been more deeply concerned. The plane was actually a U.S. Air Force E-3 Sentry aircraft that had been running a training exercise to test their systems under polar conditions. Also known as an AWACS (Advanced Warning and Control System), the aircraft, a modified Boeing 707, was designed to provide all-weather surveillance, command, control, and communications to U.S. and allied armed forces. With a large mushroom shaped radar dome on its fuselage, it was one of the most distinctive aircraft in the world. This aircraft was operating out of Australia to test latest upgrades of their surveillance systems in the one of the harshest, desolate environments in the world. Along with imaging of airborne objects, they were also examining the ability of their instruments to detect small objects within ice floes. They had "seen" the two trawlers and the cargo ship on the way out and had noted that they were probably fishing trawlers. They were not paying particular attention to the trawlers, and didn't note the disappearance of one from radar.

They had flown along the Antarctic ice pack and were now on their way back to their base in Australia. Their return course ordinarily would have taken them back on the same route. The commander of the AWACS team knew that the French navy patrolled this part of the world, which was a rich fishing ground for the Patagonian tooth fish—better known as Orange Roughy. A slow growing deepwater fish, there was much concern that its stocks could be endangered by illegal fishing. A dedicated environmentalist, the airplane commander was interested in what the fishing trawlers were up to. He could always notify the French navy about their presence. The extraordinary imaging and recording systems of the aircraft allowed them to tell much about the two ships even at 30,000 feet. He decided to request permission to alter his return course. Several hours after the initial sighting, they could not find the trawlers anywhere on the radar. It was not possible that the trawlers could have sailed out of range of the radar in that amount of time. The converted 707 dropped down in altitude to observe the area where they had been sighted more closely. They not only had extraordinary radar and signals analysis, they were also testing a new powerful digital optical system that could resolve extraordinary detail. They can also replay all of the earlier recorded data for further analysis.

They could clearly see the debris in the area from the trawlers. The pilot put out a call to the French navy to see if they might have a vessel on the island that could examine the wreckage. Their imaging in infrared wavelengths detected the presence of hydrocarbon on the sea surface indicating that there might have been a fire or at least a leak in the diesel tanks of the ships. The hydrocarbon showed up like a broad stain on the water and the debris field was extensive.

"Can you play back our scans from the trip out? I know we were working some targets on the other side and didn't pay a great deal of attention to those trawlers. Let's run it back to when we could first see them, not when the operators noticed them," asked the officer in charge of the imaging team.

"Sure thing, Captain," replied the crewman running one of the big electronic consoles. "It'll just take a minute."

The radar recording capacity of the aircraft systems was extraordinary. It could store the data from many different flights and play it back or send it electronically for more detailed analysis on the ground. It was said that the AWACS system was capable of recording an entire air war for the first time in history and play the information back for the further analysis.

The images that appeared showed the two trawlers moving across the ocean. The unknown cargo ship was farther out, almost at the horizon. Everything appeared normal.

"Now we're at the point where we first logged their presence," commented the analyst. . Even though they were not yet at the area, the radar had recorded the image of the two ships clearly.

"Uh, oh, what's that?" The target's signature suddenly increased and then faded. Only two smaller echoes showed up. "Looks like one of them blew up and the ship broke in two."

"Yep, that's definitely a break up," replied the captain. "One part is sinking faster than the other."

In minutes, both pieces were gone from the radar. The missile strike was then seen on the second trawler, followed shortly by the second strike.

"The image analysis is giving a new signal. Looks like a periscope about 500 meters away."

"Can we back track those missiles—we should be able to source them?"

"Yes, definitely not from the cargo ship. She may not even be able to see what's happening. She's far away and the weather is crappy there."

It's a periscope, sir. Stealth enhanced but we're still picking it up, it's blurry, but it has to be a submarine launch of a missile. That earlier explosion was too big, probably a torpedo.

"So we've got a submarine sinking fishing trawlers?"

"Looks like it, sir. They certainly aren't buying fish off of them," said the airman, grinning at his console.

He dialed up the base controller and related what they had seen. The E-3 made several low passes over the area to gather more imaging. The imaging file was immediately downloaded to Defense Intelligence Agency for further analysis.

This allowed the *Alistair Billings* to move rapidly away from the area. Although it couldn't outrun the AWACS, by altering course and pushing its speed to the maximum it was able to move out of the area the aircraft could cover with its radar. While not low on fuel, the aircraft could not spare time for an extensive search for the freighter. The *Alistair Billings* vanished into the mists of the Southern Oceans.

"We'll head south towards the ice pack. The icebergs should confuse them if they are really looking for us. Blain and her team will transfer over to the *Retter*. Willy, you need to steam on as fast as possible to the prearranged pick up point. I've got a feeling that this is going to get very complicated," asserted Bwana Doc.

"Och, well, we always like that best, don't we?" growled Roberson in reply. "We'll be waiting for you when you're through with your fun."

Bwana Doc clapped Willy on the back. "You're a stout one, Willy. I wish you were with me, but we'll see you soon enough."

"You've chosen a tough task for us, Bwana Doc and our fortune has been good so far; I think you'll see us through to the end safe and sound."

The old Scot had a deep and abiding affection for Bwana Doc. He had known him from the Africa days and knew more of his story than most of the confederates. He knew the reservoirs of courage and resourcefulness in this determined man and he had seen them proved many times. He had no doubts about the ultimate success of the mission.

Chapter 19

In Pursuit of a Pirate

"Crime is a logical extension of the sort of behavior that is often considered perfectly respectable in legitimate business"—Robert Rice

Bennett Boyd continued to analyze the loss of the submarine and correlate it with other information in the area. The rendezvous of the *Alistair Billings* with the *Walter Wilt* reported by the Norwegians had convinced her that it was somehow involved in the disappearance. The *Alistair Billings* stood out as an odd ship to be there at anytime. There were no petroleum deposits in the Southern Ocean in any quantity. There was no reason for the ship to be there. It could be that the refueling stop could have involved the submarine, but where was it?

Her liaison person in the Defense Intelligence Agency called. They had a small team devoted to the piracy problem and the information from the AWACS was funneled to his group. The information electrified the team. The submarine had been found! Now they knew the submarine was not only still afloat and in operation but was utilizing its weapons for no good purpose. Clearly she was not in the hands of Columbians, either. There was no reason to smuggle drugs to the Antarctic. The connection with the Alistair Billings remained unclear.

"That ship may have been the *Billings*, but the image was too poor to make sure—it is about the right size, though. DIA confirms that the periscope and missile track is consistent with

Admiral Mendoza's class of submarine. We've definitely got a rogue submarine out there and she's sinking ships" said Boyd emphatically.

Rudolf replied, "We have to look for a common denominator. Assuming the submarine was hijacked, who would need it? And for what?"

"What about those fishing trawlers? Any info on those?" queried Boyd.

"They were bought in Durban, South Africa, another shell corporation, just like the *Billings* and the *Wilt*. Went out without any fishing licenses, crew list doesn't have any one traceable, paid cash for fuel. One guy interviewed in the harbor said they went out without any fishing nets. DIA found no evidence of bodies in the wreckage in any of the images from the AWACS."

"No nets? So why did they go out?"

"Target practice?" questioned Boyd. "That would explain the lack of bodies. The ships were derelicts-- targets for gunnery."

Both of the investigators stared at each other. They knew the path of the submarine was taking it into the latest area of pirate operations.

"We need to get down there," Bennett said flatly.

It was clear that nothing more was to be gained by staying so far from the action. If they were to catch pirates, they needed to go where the pirates were.

"Tell the team we're packing our bags, we're leaving for K-L tomorrow. We'll rendezvous with the U.S.N. *Liberty* there, and then we'll go pirate hunting. That submarine had to have been headed to the center of the pirate activity," she announced. There was no other explanation. Islamic terrorists didn't need to steal that submarine. There were plenty of similar submarines in the hands of countries sympathetic to their aims if they wanted to commit some terrorist sinking. There was only one group that could benefit from acquiring such a tool of destruction and stealth.

The news was greeted with applause from the team members. They were tired of hearing of incident after incident where the pirates had again robbed a freighter, perhaps killed its crew. They were all policemen by training and they were ready to catch some bad guys.

Arriving in K-L, they met with the commander of the U.S.N. *Liberty*. The *Liberty* was a Littoral Combat Ship, designed for close to shore operations. She was a potent combat ship and one of the most advanced war vessels afloat. While capable of being configured for a variety of missions including launching assault troops for shore operations, the Liberty carried two SH-60 Seahawk helicopters and a potent mix of Mk 50 antisubmarine torpedoes, a 57 mm cannon capable of firing 200 rounds per minute, the RIM-116 Rolling Airframe Missile (RAM) for anti cruise and anti aircraft defense, and the NETFIRES Non- line of sight precision attack missile that could be used as both an antiship and anti shore attack missile. Her innovative trimaran hull was powered by a combination of two Rolls-Royce MT30 36 MW gas turbines and two Colt-Pielstick diesel engines. These drove four Rolls-Royce

D. R. Schneider

water jets that gave her a speed of over 45 knots, capable of catching just about any ship, submarine or not, in the world. With enhanced antisubmarine capabilities both on ship and in the Sea Hawk helicopters, she was ideal for the task of finding the wayward submarine even if it chose to hide in the islands off shore of Australia or in the Indonesian archipelago.

Her captain, Commander William Hayford was no stranger to these waters. He had several years of experience operating in the Persian Gulf, Indian Ocean, and South China Sea. A tall, fit, tanned sailor, he was the picture of a naval officer. Dark eyed and haired, he gazed calmly out of his bridge, sleek with high tech equipment that made his ship one of the most formidable of its type in the world. However, inside, his emotions ran hot. He was energized about a possible mission involving catching real live pirates. A student of the days of sail, he looked forward to a modern day final shoot out with this clearly ambitious group of pirates. In course of his stay in the Far and Middle East, he had seen a few ships they had raided. One in particular stayed in their memories. The pirates had taken the ship at dawn and when the captain refused to give them the combination to the safe where the crew's pay was kept, they had tortured the captain's wife and daughter in front of him. After he broke, they killed the wife and took the daughter with them. The daughter was sold into a white slavery ring. She was later found in a Thai brothel and rescued but not before she had been infected with HIV. He was still haunted by the look on the face of the captain when they had found the hijacked ship. Hayford was looking forward to finding the people that could commit a heinous crime like that.

Bennett's team boarded midday after an overnight flight from Paris to Kuala Lumpur. They carried their own weapons in bulky cases. Hayford's orders were to cooperate with her to bring about the end of the pirate organization. Bennett shook his hand and greeted him warmly. "It's a pleasure to meet you, Commander. We've been working toward this goal for a long time."

Hayford knew Boyd's naval background and respected her career. He knew that Boyd brought an extra dimension to the hunt that might be the key. They had always lacked intelligence of where the pirates were. As soon as the team had been bunked and settled in, they met with the commander and his officers in the Situation Room of the high tech ship. Bennett Boyd had carefully planned the campaign. She had all the data on pirate hijackings that had involved unusually valuable or unique cargos plotted and correlated as to time and place. They all lead to a center of activity not so much in Indonesia, but more toward Australia. The pirates appeared to be moving south and west. This made sense to Boyd and Hayford. The Indonesian and Malaysian navies had spent considerable effort in finding or infiltrating pirate gangs working along the Straits of Malacca itself. While attacks had continued, the ships that passed through the Strait had to go somewhere and that somewhere was east, south, or north. North took them toward China and South toward Australia where a resurgent mining industry was churning out a variety of rare and precious metals and minerals just perfect for the desires of pirates-- a small, valuable, and untraceable commodity to steal. Now if only their contacts within the pirate organization would give them information on their next target.

"You've heard nothing from your inside man?" Boyd queried Hayford.

"Nothing has come to us from Naval Intelligence. We're all praying he's O.K., but have no reason to think he's not. In other cases when inside operatives were found out, the pirates were very open about announcing their capture and execution. They want to intimidate their enemies. The worst thing these people can have is a turncoat, because they don't have a lot of assets to project force, they rely on surprise to capture these ships. What can you tell us about the submarine?"

"You got the same intelligence we have. She's not a bathtub toy and could probably sink any ship afloat if she caught it by surprise. She's perfect for positioning a surprise attack, of course. Even ships anchored in a roads or a harbor could be cut out by her. We don't know if this ship the *Alistair Billings* is involved with it or not. It seems too big of a coincidence that it isn't, but we don't have proof. We do know the submarine is headed into the same area where we've seen the greatest pirate incidents. That means we need to be ready if this is a new escalation of their activities. "

"A ship like that in their hands is scary," nodded Hayford. "I was in a war game exercise with boats just like these four years ago in the North Sea. We were tasked with defending oil platforms.

Those ships are so quiet; we lost several ships on paper to sneak attacks before we were able to sink them. Also, they have a very shallow draft and go into inshore water where sonar is useless to track them. Their armament is state of the art. If it really is in the hands of pirates-we're in for some difficulty for sure. We can handle it, but all hands are going to have to be on their toes." This latter remark addressed to his officers.

D. R. Schneider

Chapter 20

A New Target

"And as for the other whale, why, I'll agree to get more oil by chopping up and trying out these three masts of ours, than he'll get from that bundle of bones; though, now that I think of it, it may contain something worth a good deal more than oil; yes, ambergris."—Herman Melville, Moby Dick

"Besides all those whaling details, Moby Dick is about someone who's looking for something so huge, something they've wanted all their life, yet they know when they find it, it will kill them."--Laurie Anderson

The captain of the *Yoshino Maru*, Akira Sato, had never received such a request. The message from the Committee for Cetacean Research was astounding. Never before had the research plans of the vessel been changed during a voyage. Akira immediately called a meeting with the scientific team.

Hajime Hatamoto was the first to object. "We have our planned research on the Minke whales to carry out, if we change our target population, we won't be able to make our quota for the year. "

Akira replied, "The directive is clear—these are orders, not a request. But perhaps we can still meet our quotas. The orders state we only have to change our target species until we find the item requested."

"But who knows how long that will be? We might have to kill 20, 30, 40 whales before we find what we need.' Hatamoto injected.

"Then we'll have a new topic to present a scientific paper on— the frequency of ambergris in sperm whale intestines," asserted Akira.

Hatamoto still was obstinate. "I must contact headquarters directly on this subject."

"Please, doctor, feel free," Akira replied. "This isn't my idea; I'm only passing on orders. Another point, I don't believe anyone outside of the ship and the catchers will know—the Oceanwarriors boats are disabled and the Australians have left us—we have the ocean to ourselves.

Hatamoto's query via e-mail was quickly done and the answer was swift. "Change research to sperm whales and capture until fresh ambergris is found."

Hatamoto was nothing if not a good employee. He gave orders to his team, "Consult the literature at once and find what ages of sperm whales are most likely to have ambergris present. We are hunting sperm whales now."

What little evidence they could find, as ambergris finds were not regularly recorded, suggested that older bull whales tended to have more ambergris—possibly because they were ill. This made the hunt harder. Bulls often were solitary animals and were not with the families of cows and calves. However, because they were that much larger, they could be identified unambiguously on the imaging sonar and radar that the *Yoshino Maru* and the catcher ships carried. The hunt began. They had sighted several pods of sperm whales in the past week and so they had an idea of where to begin their search.

They soon located a likely prey. It was deep, as sperm whales hunt deep for their food. The passive sonar of the *Yoshino Maru* could hear the echo locating pings of the large male. These are loud, one of the loudest sounds on Earth, and many scientists believed that they used this loud sound to stun their prey, the large squid and fish that they ate. The catcher boats had to wait for the whale to sound or come to the surface for sperm whales can stay submerged for up to fifty minutes. Patience is always rewarded and eventually the big bull came to the surface. He was harpooned and killed in short order by one of the catcher boats. He was winched aboard the *Yoshino Maru* and was promptly cut open. Removal of the blubber and the spermaceti were secondary tasks. The whale's intestines were removed and cut open but the search for ambergris was unsuccessful. Only its last meal of squid was found. Then the carcass was surrendered to the cutting of blubber. The spermaceti was bailed out into improvised containers, some large bulk plastic totes that had been brought along to carry fruit juice for the crew. The large conical teeth found in the lower jaw were removed— prized items in the markets of Asia.

They continued to hunt sperm whales the rest of the day. They deliberately avoided killing cows that were believed to have a lower likelihood of having ambergris. The day ended with a total of four sperm whales taken, and no ambergris.

Hashimoto met with his staff in the evening. He posed them the question, "How can we improve the likelihood of finding the ambergris we need?"

Tadashi Imagawa, one of his younger researchers and on his first whaling trip raised his hand, "I have been reading the old whaling

157

accounts from the 19th century. There was a belief that ambergris was produced by sick whales."

"Aha", said Hashimoto, "But how do we find sick whales?"

"It would stand to reason that sick whales would spend more time on the surface where it is warmer and they don't have to expend as much energy. We could initiate a radar search looking for whales that seem to stay on the surface much longer. With the catcher vessels radar also in use, we could cover a very large area," Imagawa replied.

"An excellent idea! It should be possible to obtain recordings of the radar imaging and analyze it as we go along. A similar system has been used to track bird populations" Hashimoto remarked enthusiastically.

"Yes, and I believe we have software that will search those images and find us likely targets that can be checked out," added Imagawa.

The team nodded vigorously, liking the plan. Hashimoto immediately spoke to the captain who confirmed that the team could get records of the radar imaging for the last several days. The analysis could be begun immediately. The group of scientists went to work.

By morning the exhausted team could verify at least three possible targets. One of the catchers was sent to each of the targets. One turned out to be a dead whale. The other two were rapidly harpooned and killed, one a cow, the other a bull. In the cow, they found what they were looking for—a large smelly gray mass from its intestines. It weight over 10 kilograms—worth a small fortune on the open market, but far more to the private buyer—but of course they knew nothing of that. Samples were taken and preserved in liquid nitrogen and then the entire mass was quick frozen in a large plastic case.

Hashimoto was overjoyed. In only three days, they had found what they were looking for—the Director General would be pleased. He emailed their success off immediately. The reply was rapid. "Stand by, we will send transport for the ambergris."

Pleased with his success, with no real interruption in their program, the Yoshino Maru could now return to killing Minkes. It had harvested only six sperm whales and completed their goal of finding the fresh ambergris. They had not even deviated from the IWC quota (which was not really a quota—the Japanese set their own quotas). No one would know what had transpired.

D. R. Schneider

Chapter 21

Pirates on the Move—Pursuit on the High Seas

"Merchant and pirate were for a long period one and the same person. Even today mercantile morality is really nothing but a refinement of piratical morality." --Friedrich Nietzsche

Poolom Pannarang was not used to the confined space of the submarine. He felt the urge to leap into the water to get out of the steel tube that he was in, and every minute the boat was on the surface he could be found on the sail bridge, enjoying the air that was getting colder and colder as they sailed south. He would rather be on the *Labah-Labah*, but he knew that he had to be in on the greatest coup of his career, the triumph that would give him respect and fear throughout the world. Vladimir and his crew were as expected sullen and moody. They were making good time and the submarine was performing perfectly as they sailed at full speed south. They stayed on the surface for the most part and only submerged when their radar detected another vessel. They had no need to travel as rapidly as possible as they were awaiting word from Gamali that the ambergris had been secured. The ride was rougher on the surface and the temperature was steadily going colder. They had picked up their additional armament and the crew along with Jessica Tate. Twenty of Poolom's most trusted and ruthless men who were anticipating the action also accompanied them.

D. R. Schneider

The Kilo class submarine was a formidable instrument. One of the quietest diesel electric submarines ever made by the former Soviet Union, it had first entered service in the early 1980s. With a water drop shaped double hull covered with anechoic rubber tiles and a T-shaped stern rudder, she had six watertight compartments. The command and fire control stations in the main control room could be sealed off from the other compartments. Her single seven bladed propeller could drive her at 20 knots underwater and 12 knots on the surface. Her armament was also substantial. The resourceful Gamali had acquired from the Indonesian navy six Model 53-66 wake homing torpedoes. Owning a couple of submarines in the Russian Kilo class had made the Indonesians a natural source of supply of weapons for the pirate submarine These lethal torpedoes carried a passive sonar system that would follow the wake of the ship until they reached their target. Powered by a kerosene oxygen turbine, they were highly effective once they acquired a signal. Traveling at 45 knots and a range of 18,000 meters and carrying a 300 kilogram explosive charge she could sink any ship that sailed the ocean. He had been unable to obtain any large anti ship missiles that could be launched from the submarine's torpedo tubes, but he had been able to obtain some hand fired missiles that could be launched from the deck. These would be ideal for sinking the catcher ships and could also be used against aircraft if necessary. Vladimir had some men skilled in servicing the torpedoes and they were put to work on the ordinance now, glad to put their long unused military skills to work. The work went on as they waited for word that the Japanese had acquired the ambergris and they drove relentlessly toward the whaling fleet, undetected by anyone.

Back in Paris, Chevillac received word of the successful harvesting of the ambergris with jubilation. She immediately called Lampin who happened to be working with Amelie Broussard. Lampin was equally enthusiastic—his product was one step closer to completion. Amelie asked what had happened and he could not restrain himself from telling her. Amelie smiled to herself. Yes, this was a very good day—she would get enough money for this to buy a house in the country outright and probably a very nice car as well. It was a very good day for her indeed.

Bwana Doc was getting close to the whaling vessels. Although satellite imaging for this part of the world was spotty at best and clouds frequently obscured visual data, he knew from the planned area of harvest that he was getting close. A contact in Oceanwarriors had also proven helpful in this regard. Their vessels were close to having its repairs completed and Bwana Doc had to move quickly before they would arrive and complicate matters for him. The weather was becoming predictably worse and colder. They spent most of their days submerged. They were staying out of the ice floes as much as possible, but he knew they would have to go further south to find the Japanese fleet.

The *Billings* would wait in the harbor of Hobart, Tasmania and would pick them up once the mission was completed. The drilling ship would be perfect cover for his getaway. It was likely that the world would know that a submarine had destroyed the whaling fleet, but it would not know that the *Alistair Billings* was involved with it in any way. He knew that he would have future use of the submarine and did not want to abandon it if at all possible.

The weather had worsened and the submarine spent most of its time submerged. The floe ice was still spotty and they easily detected any large ice bergs in their path with the sonar. When they surfaced just to give the crew a change to get some fresh air, the wind rocked the sail of the submarine and whistled through the open hatches, chilling the conn station below the sail.

Bwana Doc had laid his plans carefully. He had not yet killed anyone on a mission except in self defense and he planned his attack on the *Yoshino Maru* accordingly. Once they found the whaling fleet, the plan would be to use relay radio buoy to send a radio message telling the *Yoshino Maru* to abandon ship or be sunk. This way, the radio signal could not be traced back to the submarine. He would also call the ship's satellite phone and tell the captain via a recorded Japanese message that his ship would be sunk if he did not abandon it immediately. Likewise an untraceable email was sent through a Tor connection and sent to the ship's captain. If no response was received or no positive response, he would then initiate a demonstration of his ability to sink the ship that hopefully would get them to abandon the *Yoshino Maru*. If that failed, then he would then board the ship.

Poolom Pannarang had no such scruples. He already had his simple ruthless plan in mind from the first day he had heard of the project. Attack the ship with zodiacs deployed from the submarine, board her, take the ambergris and then use the submarine to sink the *Yoshino Maru* and any catcher ships that had seen the submarine. He could then head to his base in Indonesia, deliver the ambergris and get paid. He figured that boarding the ship first and capturing her was the most likely way to get the ambergris unharmed. The Japanese would certainly expect to be boarded with none of the environmentalists in sight and far from the shipping lanes associated with piracy. They would be caught completely by surprise when his band of cutthroats came onto the ship using the open stern ramp used for hauling the whales on board. When he received the satellite call from Gamali that the ambergris had been found by the Japanese he pressed the submarine's engines to the limit and wasted no time in bringing himself into range of the whaling fleet.

Unknown to Bwana Doc and the Malay pirate, the environmentalists of Oceanwarriors were not without their own plan for the whaling ships. Sander had his ships underway and they were also nearing the whaling grounds. The environmentalists had argued long and hard about what they would do when they found the whalers and had decided that this time they would board the *Yoshino Maru* and take out the ship by any means possible. They had spent their time while in harbor for repair from the sabotage buying what weapons they could get either legally or illegally and now had a formidable, if somewhat motley assemblage of firepower. They were now in a frenzy to revenge themselves on the Japanese, convinced that the Japanese government was now actively supporting the whaling fleet. Sander had felt humiliated and that he had lost control of the mission. Many criticized him for not setting better guards around the ships. Although he was personally timid about physical violence, he knew that something had to be done to bring the group back under his control again and the only way to do that was to accomplish something concrete in stopping the whalers.

His plan? Board the ship however possible and use their own fire hoses to hold the crew at bay while they came aboard. Once there they would either set the ship ablaze with homemade Molotov cocktails they were making or if they could do it, sink the ship by opening her sea cocks.

Sander had crafted his own plan to come out the front page environmental hero he had always wanted to be and if it involved the loss of some of his shipmates and a few of his ships, well that was too bad. Too long he had played the game of press release and casual harassment—finally he had been pushed into actually doing something dangerous. He would make sure he wouldn't be the one doing it, but he would get the credit for it.

The Japanese, however, were well aware of the preparations of the Oceanwarriors' fleet. The ever observant and dedicated Lieutenant Naru Shan had returned early and had spent his evenings at the Dockside Bar and Restaurant well. He had seen the ominous looking cases that could fit some type of a gun come aboard. The police after a couple of weeks of guarding the pier had slacked off on their patrolling. They were not really wanted by the Oceanwarriors crews in any case as the police might interfere with some of their less salubrious forms of recreation that they tended to engage in. He also had seen the arrival of what appeared to be gasoline cans on board, even though he knew that all of the environmentalist's ships were diesel powered. The crewmen were also busy installing water cannons on the ships.

The Oceanwarriors were now vigilant with regular guards posted on each of the ships. Roane Sander also hired a private security firm to augment his own people as he didn't trust the police. Shan saw no opportunity to stop the ships from sailing this time so he informed his headquarters as to the apparent intentions of the Oceanwarriors' fleet.

The Japanese government responded with alacrity. The tough nationalist prime minister would stop at nothing to protect Japanese ships—especially fishing ships that caught the fish that was so much a part of the Japanese lifestyle and culture. He immediately instructed the Japanese Navy to protect the whalers with all means possible—including lethal force. The Committee for Cetacean Research also added an additional request that was also relayed to the Japanese naval vessel that was closest to the whalers.

The Japanese navy "*Kongō* class" guided missile destroyer *Chokai* was on an extended Pacific cruise and was docked in Rabaul, New Guinea. Lieutenant Commander Imadura Tonga immediately set sail for the Southern Ocean to rendezvous with the whaling ships. Excepting the Liberty, she was easily the fastest ship in the collection of vessels headed toward the whaling fleet. She was also technically sophisticated. The *Kongō* class of guided missile destroyers, a modification of the United States Navy *Arleigh Burke* class employed the highly advanced Aegis fire control system. She was armed with the RIM-66 SM-2 Block II surface-to-air missile, the RUM-139 vertically launched anti-submarine rocket, the RGM-84 Harpoon anti-ship missile, two Mark 15 20 mm CIWS (close in weapon system) gun mounts. The latter were sometimes referred to as R2D2s for their resemblance to the Star Wars robot. If these were not enough they also had two torpedo mounts in a triple tube configuration, and an Oto Melara 127 mm/54 caliber gun. Its Mark 41 vertical launch system held ninety missiles. She was a lethal ship.

Tonga was no great fan of the whaling ships. He thought the killing of whales a barbarous and economically unprofitable activity. He equally disliked the environmentalists. They were truly little better than pirates and should be sunk. His orders were clear. Protect the whaling vessels from environmental pirates and take off an important item to be kept under refrigeration and arrange its transport back to Japan for study. He had stopped in port to refuel and restock his ship and so was able to sail almost immediately for the rendezvous with the *Yoshino Maru* and her catcher boats.

Jessica now knew the full plan of Pannerang and she was desperate to communicate with the Navy. She had tried several times to use the radio equipment of the submarine to send a message, but had been interrupted repeatedly by Russian crew members on the crowded boat. She took a chance on a midnight watch in the submarine's radio shack while the submarine was running on the surface. Many of those on watch were taking turns up on the cool deck getting some fresh air. She had befriended the Russian radio operator and was able to talk Vladimir into allowing her access to the equipment in order to continue to monitor for the position of the whaling fleet and other possible targets. She took the chance to send a brief radio message on the frequency always monitored by naval intelligence. Using her code name, Vibra, she gave the location, course and plan for the pirates. "Vibra, in submarine with pirates, position 121 degrees East, 42 degrees South, heading 110 degrees South by East, Japanese whalers."

She only had time to send the transmission three times and she was interrupted on the last try. The radio operator had not made any special comment as he was glad to have a break and a chat with the only woman on board. Jessica gave a special smile to the man and had deliberately stayed longer to talk with him. Tension had grown on the pirate submarine as they approached their latest victim. The prospect of murder and mayhem in particular especially heightened the anticipation among the Malay members of the crew. The Russians, who were really only in it for the money, could have cared less about what would be done to the crew of the Japanese whaler, but they were very interested in their share of the profits.

D. R. Schneider

Harwood received the report from Naval Intelligence on Jessica's whereabouts and activity with astonishment. That the pirates had a submarine, although suspected, still came as a shock to have it confirmed. He immediately told the news to Boyd and within hours the *Liberty* was at sea and sailing south at full speed.

Naval Intelligence also relayed the information to the Japanese government. The Japanese government, thinking the Americans were referring to the environmental pirates informed them that they already knew about the threat and had a naval ship in route. The submarine part of the message was not understood and as no follow-up message was received, they concluded that submarine might refer somehow to how the Americans had learned of the pirate threat. Somewhat nonplussed by the reply, the Americans concluded they had done their duty and focused on the activity of their own ship.

Bwana Doc, unaware of the confusion that was growing between the various ships headed for the whaling fleet finally located the flotilla on radar. Ever methodical, he developed his plan slowly and carefully. The radio buoy was deployed and the signal for the *Yoshino Maru* to abandon ship was delivered. He kept the *Retter* submerged and traveling on electric power alone, not wanting to risk detection by the fairly sophisticated sonars of the whaling fleet.

Used to harassment by environmentalists, the Japanese whaling captain ignored the warnings, thinking they were coming from the Oceanwarriors' ships or perhaps some other group of protesters.

He had been informed that the ships had been repaired and were on their way. The Japanese whalers immediately sent a message to Japan asking for help and was informed with gratifying speed that help had already been dispatched in the form of the frigate *Chokai*. The captain was pleased and this made him a bit complacent. His crew had responded well to the challenge to procure the ambergris. From the news of the frigate on the way, he was sure that this year the environmentalists would be stopped for good. The hunting had been excellent even with the diversion of the ambergris quest and they were well on their way to completing their quota. He understood from the company that the *Chokai* would be taking off the ambergris, relieving him of that burden as well. Content with all the news he had heard, he decided that the crew could use a break from the hard working of killing and cutting up whale bodies. He declared tomorrow a day of rest. He had the crew clean up the last kill early and use the water hoses to clean the deck. In the chill air, a couple of barrels of sake were breeched, beer brought out of stores and all hands were allowed to partake to celebrate a successful year so far. The captain disclosed the assistance of the *Chokai* that was on the way. Both the crew and the scientists greeted this with general enthusiasm. If the Oceanwarriors pirates could be put out of the way once and for all, the ship could harvest its quota quicker each year and the men could be back with their families that much sooner.

The crew partied well into the light gloom that passed for an Antarctic night. The two men standing watch on the bridge were envious of their colleague's celebration, but they had been able to have a drink or two of sake before going on duty, so they were content that they had not entirely missed the celebration. The sea was quiet with an increase in the number of ice floes, but none of a size that threatened the ship. The radar operator had also set the system on an automatic warning mode of large ice in the water if he failed to see them himself. The ship was making just enough headway to keep station in the current. The catcher boats were all over the horizon where a large pod of whales had been sighted late the day before.

Chapter 22

Captured by Pirates!

"The modern day pirate could be a group of desperate ex-fisherman carrying machetes and the odd pistol or two, coming onboard to steal whatever they can get there hands on: the odd mooring rope, a can of paint or two and if they are lucky the gold watch that the Boson wears. Or they could be a highly organized bunch of professionals armed to the teeth with machine guns, wearing camouflage and prepared to kill at the drop of a hat. These latter groups are not after the odd can of paint, they may be after the cargo that the ship carries in its holds or tanks and even after the ship itself."-- Ieuan Dolby

No one noticed the pirate submarine surface directly astern to the *Yoshino Maru*. The submarine had surfaced too close to the ship to be picked up on the radar. Poolom Pannarang had prepared his team of twenty men, his most savage and skilled Malay pirates.

Jessica knew that she had to get off of the submarine and get on the factory ship if she was going to do anything to prevent its destruction. She didn't have a plan, but she couldn't allow all those people to die without doing something.

"Poolom," she asked quietly, "Do you think I could go along? You know, the Japanese have the best electronics—we might be able to pick up some things to use in the rest of our ships or maybe sell."

Poolom looked at his electronic spy genially. He could feel success in his veins and was feeling magnanimous. "Certainly, my dear. You are as good with a knife and a gun as these cutthroats. And I trust you more in any case."

"I've already got my 9 millimeter ready to go and some nice throwing knives," flashing her white teeth in a shark-like smile.

Pannarang laughed, showing his white teeth as well. "We have a great future together, Jessica. I want you by my side. After this triumph, the sky is the limit!"

He walked back through the submarine to check whether his men were prepared. All were armed with either pistols or Fabrique Nationale P90 compact submachine guns. As a matter of course, they also carried knives. They were not expecting much resistance from the fishermen. Although the crew of the Japanese ship was fairly large, they hopefully would be caught by surprise and would be unarmed.

"Are you all ready?" he barked at his men.

They all nodded and raised their hands in a fist, yelling out loud. "Poolom, Poolom, Poolom."

"Vladimir, have your men prepare the boats."

Two Zodiac inflatables had been rigged on the deck. These were now lowered into the water and ladders slung from the deck. The pirates clambered out the forward hatch of the submarine and into the boats. Jessica and Poolom climbed down into the aft boat.

"Vladimir. Submerge as planned. I don't want anyone seeing the submarine. Just keep the radio aerial up."

The Russian nodded. "Will do. And good luck!"

The Zodiacs motored off silently powered by electric outboards. Although their battery power would not last long, it did not have to

174

and the *Yoshino Maru* was making such slow headway they would have no problem reaching her.

The pirates clambered aboard the two craft which loosed their lines and began their short trip to the ship.   Behind them the submarine sank slowly beneath the waves, but kept to periscope depth where Vladimir kept a close watch on the assault on the assault in case they might need assistance or be taken off in a hurry.

The Zodiacs motored to the stern of the whaler.   One of the pirates leaped aboard the slipway and scrambled up.   A line was thrown to him and tied fast on a bollard.   The pirates pulled hard on the line and beached themselves on the slipway.   As soon as they were on the steel deck of the slipway they ran forward.   All men were assigned to a task.   The first team had the job of taking the crew and the scientists prisoner.   The second craft would take the bridge and take the officers hostage.   They all spread forward.   No shots were to be fired unless necessary.   Killing could always be done later.   Two men from the first team went down into the ship through a door.   They would find the crew and scientist quarters and report back by radio.   Three other men went down an aft gangway and headed down looking for the engine room.   It was not expected that it would be heavily manned at this hour and they were correct.   They surprised an assistant engineer and a crewman idly reading magazines while the engines rumbled away at a low RPM. The two were quickly tied up. One of the men signaled to Poolom, "Engine room is ours."

The other men soon found the sleeping quarters in the fore section of the ship. With loud shouts, the crewmen and scientist were tumbled out of their bunks and cabins. Asleep, hung over and half clothed, they were easily cowed into submission.

In the meantime, Poolom, Jessica and the other team had not been idle. They entered a hatch below the bridge and climbed rapidly and silently in the dimly lit ship. Reaching the room directly behind the bridge, they ran through and surprised the watch officer and helmsman. Rapidly clubbed into submission, the bridge was soon Poolom's. All that remained was the officer's quarters. Leaving one man with Poolom and Jessica, the rest of the pirates hurried to the aft section of the bridge superstructure where the officer's quarters were usually found. The sound of scuffles and blows soon was heard through the bridge.

They had missed the radio operator in a room directly below the bridge. He heard the running of feet and the cry of the helmsman as he was hit behind the ear with a gun butt. He reacted instinctively and shut the door to his room quietly and then began broadcasting an SOS interspersed with the words "*Yoshino Maru* under attack, *Yoshino Maru* under attack." Within minutes, he was speaking with the communications officer of the *Chokai*. The radioman got off the position of the ship but could give them no information on the attackers. The *Chokai* was not far away, but not close enough to render aid.

Poolom had the ship. He was exultant. Now to find the ambergris, deal with crew and be off. There was no reason to wait around. "Bring me the captain and the 1ˢᵗ mate," he ordered one of the men on the bridge with him.

Vladimir put a damper on his celebration as his voice came over Poolom's headset. "We're picking up a radio transmission from the *Yoshino Maru*. It's a distress call and there seems to have been a response."

Poolom slammed his hand into bulkhead and let loose a string of Malay expletives. "Jessica, take Tenang and find the radio station and cut it off."

The two sprang from the room. Jessica beckoned toward the lower stairway—"The leads from the antennas go down this way. I think it is back here." The two ran down the stairs. Not reading Japanese, they were at a loss and simply began opening doors and looking in. Finally they found a door that was closed, they listened and could hear the sound of the radio. Tenang swung the door open and they saw the extensive radio equipment talking out loudly in Japanese. Tenang entered first and as he did Jessica hit him hard on the back of the head with a sock full of lead shot. The pirate crumpled to the deck. The radio operator cowered behind the door. Jessica pointed her pistol and beckoned to the radio operator who answered back in English. "Don't shoot me, please." "Put that radio on 11175 Hz and call for the U.S. Navy. Do it now. The operator for Diego Garcia came on line. "I don't have much time, Pirates have taken the *Yoshino Maru*. They have a submarine. We need help fast. This is code name Vibra. You have maybe an hour at most to help us. Over and out."

Jessica turned off the power to the radio and spoke to the radio operator. "Turn around," she demanded. The man, cowed by the pistol in her hand did as he was told. She hit him hard, knocking him out as she had Tenang. She keyed her radio headset on. "It's off. The radio operator decked Tenang. He's out now too."

"Good, get back up here. We've got to find the ambergris and get out of here as soon as possible," replied Poolom.

The short summer gloom that passed for night in the Antarctic was coming to an end. The pirates had struck during the two hours of twilight but now the cold sun worked its way over the horizon.

Captain Sato and his first mate were on their knees before Poolom. "If you want to live, you need to tell me where the ambergris is."

The captain had no problem telling him. He wasn't about to die for any pile of expensive whale dung. "It's in the hold, stored with the whale meat. We placed it in a bright yellow box."

"Show us," demanded Poolom.

"The crew will have to open the hold."

A few crewmen were put to work opening the hatches to the hull and the bright yellow box was soon manhandled up from the frigid freezer hold of the ship. Poolom had the captain open the box. A large pile of congealed gray ooze lay in the box.

"This is what they want?" he mused aloud. "It looks like crap."

Jessica said, "That's it. That's what it looks like"

"O.K., let's get it out of here as soon as possible. Jessica, take two men and smash that radio setup. Shoot up the dishes and anything else that looks like they could use to communicate with. Any satellite phones you see lying around—dump them over the side. Men, lock the crew up in the hold. You can take what you can find of value. Get Tenang on board the Zodiac."

Jessica and the two men recovered the still unconscious Tenang and Jessica used his submachine gun to fire at the radio, carefully taking aim as she did so.

All of the pirates had finished robbing the crew and taking what money and valuables they could find on board. This was their custom and Poolom would not deny it to them even though the big prize was the ambergris. This did however, delay their leaving.

Suddenly one of the crew rummaging through a locker on the bridge looked up and saw a fleet of ships in the distance. He let out a cry, "Ships on the horizon!"

It was the ships of the Oceanwarriors. Repaired and ready for vengeance, they were heading at full speed for the *Yoshino Maru*. Nothing would stop them this time. The pirate yelled a warning to the pirates milling about as they pushed the Japanese crew down into the hold of the ship, along with the frozen boxes of whale meat.

Poolom looked up from the chest of ambergris. He thought at first that catcher ships had returned. They were in fact on their way back, having also heard the distress call, but were too far out away from the factory ship to reach her in time.

"At that rate they are going they are going to be here in minutes. We need to get out of here now!" Poolom yelled.

D. R. Schneider

Jessica used the general confusion to duck into a storage locker. She had no intention of getting back on the submarine. She had taken Tenang's submachine gun and his spare magazines and cradled it in her arms. She had been careful to shoot around the radio and it hopefully would still function. Poolom's men crowded on to the Zodiacs. In the confusion, no one missed Jessica. Soon they were at sea and they could see the submarine rising from the waves.

Roane Sander' long black hair flew in the cold Arctic air. They would soon be at the whale killer's ship. Although personally frightened, he felt swept along by the emotions of his fellow environmentalists. Radios crackled as the ships made comments and exhortations between themselves. Then he sighted the submarine behind the *Yoshino Maru*. It could only be a Japanese submarine that had come to protect the Japanese ships. This put a new complexion on matters. Warships were trained to kill and Roane Sander was not a particularly brave man. He reduced the speed of his ship slightly and let Hank Kohler's *Extreme Environment* pull into the lead.

Bwana Doc had picked up all the radio traffic and one of Blain's men knew Japanese. He had not intercepted Jessica's latest message, however. He didn't know what was going on and suspected it was the Oceanwarriors vessels actually attacking the *Yoshino Maru*. He raced toward the embattled factory ship and soon could see the other submarine on the surface.

His eyes widened as he and Blain looked at the viewing screen from the camera on the periscope. "Another submarine! Who's she with? Is she Japanese? She's flying a black flag and has no markings. She's a pirate submarine. They must be the attackers of the *Yoshino Maru*."

Bwana Doc knew well the depredations of the pirates of the Malacca Strait and the Indian Ocean. He had never heard of them operating this far south. Clearly things had taken a serious turn and matters were going to get ugly fast. He saw the men in the Zodiacs dock with the submarine and carry the large yellow box onto the deck and put it down the torpedo hatch of the submarine. As the men boarded the submarine he saw her turn toward the fleet of small vessels steaming toward the *Yoshino Maru*.

Back on the submarine, Poolom Pannarang gave his orders to Vladimir. "None of these ships or their crews can survive. If they do, the secret of the submarine will be out."

"Well, best we take out these little ships first. There are a lot of them and one might get away. "Pauli," he told his second in command, "get the missile crews up on deck. It's time for some target practice."

The men began lugging the heavy missile systems up through the fore deck hatch. The heavy European made "Milan ER (extended range)" anti-tank missiles were not state of the art, but still were lethal weapons. Guided by a wire spooled out from the rocket, they were steered to their target by one of the crew using an optical finder system. The crewmen set up the two launchers on the fore deck. In short order they were ready to fire. Although not greatly experienced on the system, Ali Mohammed Gamali's supplier had given them a crash course on their use. It took awhile, but that brought the Oceanwarriors' ships in close. They fired the first missile at the closest ship—Hank Kohler's *Extreme Environment*.

Heywood Dowd was not in the engine room where he belonged on his new ship. He decided he wasn't going to miss any of the action this time. He had spent long enough down in that hot smelly hold. So he saw the launch of the missile from the deck of the submarine and could see the small speck fly high in the air. His mouth open, he gawked as it curved and swooped downwards and hit dead on the bridge of the converted fishing trawler. Exploding, it knocked Dowd to the deck and killed everyone on the bridge instantly. Flaming debris landed around the gas cans lined up on the working deck of the converted fish trawler. The ship exploded in a roar of flames. Dowd jumped into the freezing water that stung him like he had been burned by the exploding gas. His body began to numb almost immediately from the extraordinarily cold water. Seconds later, her main fuel tanks went up in flames and she began to sink. Dowd was dead within minutes, killed by hypothermia along with the few members of the crew who had managed to jump in with him. Hank Kohler made it to the life raft on top of the bridge and managed to clamber in. He was the only survivor.

The Oceanwarriors' fleet stopped dead in the water, aghast at what they had seen. They were ready to threaten violence, but seeing the violence of modern technology in action gave them second thoughts. "We need to get out of here, they mean to sink us!" Sander yelled into his radio.

"We can't let them sink those ships." Bwana Doc exclaimed. "Captain Lavigna, give me a strong sonar ping directed at that Russian ship and get the weapons on line. I think we're going to need them."

"We're picking up a helicopter on radar. Don't know where it's from as I don't see any ship on radar. It should be within view in about 10 minutes," said the Israeli sailor manning the electronics console. "I'm not picking up any ship's screws on sonar except the sub and the *Yoshino Maru*."

Bennett Boyd and her team were in the SH-60 Seawolf helicopter from the *Liberty*. The pilot could see the submarine on radar along with the *Yoshino Maru* and the Oceanwarriors' fleet. The explosion of the *Extreme Environment* took them all by surprise. They had received the relayed message from the naval base at Diego Garcia and realized that the *Liberty* probably could not make it there in time. After consultation with Hayford, they decided to pack the helicopter with Bennett Boyd's team and a team of Marines that they had on board. They had ten good fighting men in the helicopter.

Another Oceanwarriors' vessel was hit by a missile, this one in the stern. Her engine dead, she slowly began to drop in the water.

The submarine picked up speed, not wanting any of the ships to get away and began to move away from the Japanese ship. The

D. R. Schneider

Milan missiles did not have a long range. The *Edward Abbey*, the fastest of the ships began to slip away. Vladimir directed the crews to fire at it. One missile exploded in the water next to her, spraying the ship with shrapnel and rocking her severely. Cut by some of the flying metal, blood streaming across his terrified face, Roane Sander didn't know what to do. He decided perhaps zigzagging would help and he tracked his vessel in wild erratic arcs across the freezing water.

The powerful sonar ping from the *Retter* had brought Vladimir and Poolom up short and saved the remaining environmental ships. Vladimir ordered all engines to stop, knowing that their sound would guide any torpedoes straight to his boat. At the same time, they detected the helicopter coming in on radar. It was clear from its signature that it was probably a military helicopter.

"We've got company and probably trouble. That's a military helicopter headed this way. It can carry both missiles and torpedoes that can sink us on the surface or underwater. We know that the whalers got off a distress call. We don't have weapons for a submarine that is not underway. The torpedoes we have are wake guided, they home in on the noise of the propellers. They'll only pick up surface vessels that are underway. With her engines off line, we can only sink the *Yoshino Maru* by firing directly at her. " Vladimir informed Poolom.

"Can you take out the helicopter?" Poolom demanded.

"Maybe, if we can get her in close. I'll need a visual. The missile has the range. The *Yoshino Maru* is between us and the

184

helicopter—we'll use her as a screen. If they are here to protect her, they won't fire on us if we're close enough.

On board the *Yoshino Maru*, Jessica had been busy releasing the crew from the hold. Angry at the pirates, they were out for blood. Soon they had the ship's engines turning over again. As the submarine drew closer to the ship, the angry captain ordered the ship to be prepared for full speed. He signaled the catcher ships to come in as quickly as possible. If the submarine was that close, there was something they could do to stop it. He ordered two crewmen to go to the stores and bring out some spare items that they kept in stock.

In the Sea Wolf helicopter, the team was ready to rappel down to the *Yoshino Maru*. The pilot had also activated his weapons systems in case they might be needed. Bennett Boyd strained to see exactly what was going on. When she saw the submarine she naturally assumed that it was the *Admiral Mendoza* as all modern submarines for the most part look alike—bulbous, guppy shaped hulls with a tall aerodynamic sail superstructure on the fore of the vessel.

Bwana Doc was now in position to attack either the *Yoshino Maru* or the submarine, but he had no quarrel with the crew of either. He only wanted to sink the ship. He told Blain and her team to get ready.

"If we have to retake the *Yoshino Maru* to save the crew, we will. I'm willing to bet that helicopter is from a U.S. or Japanese naval vessel here to free the crew from those pirates. We may need to help them do that. No one is going to die if I can help it."

Jessica Tate had made it back to the radio room of the *Yoshino Maru*. Her aim had been good. The radio still worked. Talking to the *Liberty*, she learned of the Seawolf helicopter on the way. Soon she was talking to pilot of the helicopter letting him know that the crew had been freed and all of the pirates were on board the submarine.

Another missile flew at the environmentalist fleet. At the far edge of the Milan's range, it exploded in mid air, showering Clare Wood's *Rachel Carson* with shrapnel. The gasoline tanks on deck were pierced and caught on fire. The crew fought it fiercely with the fire extinguishers that they had and soon had it under control. They continued their escape from the missile barrage of the pirates.

Vladimir now ordered his men to target the helicopter. Both crews fired almost simultaneously and the two missiles shot off the deck of the submarine, headed straight for the Seawolf.

"Incoming missiles!" yelled the pilot over the intercom as he sent the helicopter in a stomach-emptying dive bringing it right down to the surface of the ocean. He also fired flare countermeasures to confuse the missiles. However the missiles were guided by wires and were immune to such countermeasures. They plunged down toward the helicopter. The pilot pulled the big helicopter into a steep climb bringing it up toward the descending missile. Then he jinxed sharp to the right, just missing it. Its tracking devices unable to react in time, the missile plunged into the ocean.

However the second missile was already at the helicopter. It flashed through the spinning rotor blades where a blade cut through the body of the missile exploding the remaining propellant and sending the warhead of the missile tumbling to the ocean.

Damaged by the impact, the rotor blades began to come apart under the stress. The pilot throttled down the motor, to reduce the stress on the unbalanced blades and began to look for a place to land. Landing in the water was not an option. The freezing Antarctic water would kill them all within minutes. The only ships large enough to land on were the pirate submarine and the *Yoshino Maru*. As the submarine could clearly submerge beneath them, he opted for the latter—a larger ship in any case. He put the damaged helicopter into a shallow dive and headed for the Japanese whaler!

D. R. Schneider

Chapter 23

The End of the *Yoshino Maru*

Japan's scientific study has also revealed that whales consume some 500 million tonnes of fish resources per year (up to six times total human consumption). The bulk of this is consumed by non-endangered whale species. This knowledge is useful in helping to plan ways to sustainably feed the world's population. Fishing will become increasingly important in this task (particularly given the environmental problems caused by the massive amounts of land clearing and deforestation going on to produce red meat). With about 35% of the world's fishery resources already over-exploited and another 25% exploited to their fullest extent, the role of whales in the ecosystem should be carefully considered.—from the Institute for Cetacean Research website.

The captain of the *Yoshino Maru* had not been idle. He knew that the submarine must be planning to sink his ship now that they had gotten what they had come for. His crew had rigged the spare harpoon gun on the railing along with a length of cable attached to it. Taking aim they fired at two of the men that were holding one of the missile launchers. The barbed harpoon stuck the metal deck and the three kilogram charge exploded, blowing a large hole in the coating, spraying rubber fragments everywhere. The missile boxes were narrowly missed but the launcher and targeting system was upset and badly damaged. The two Russians were knocked to the deck senseless from the force of the explosion. The steel hull of the submarine was mangled and the harpoon remained stuck in the hull, the attached cable still on the whaling ship.

Sato set his crew to work. They spliced the end of the harpoon cable onto the cable attached to one of the winches used for bringing the whales on board for butchering. They began to reel the cable in, the powerful motors straining under this, the largest "whale" the *Yoshino Maru* had ever caught. The submarine swung in the water under the force of the pull of the cable.

"The cable won't take the strain, Captain. That submarine is too big," yelled the winch engine operator.

"Give it some slack, then!" yelled the Captain, "Just don't let it get away." The cable paid out and went slack in the water, relieving the strain.

Vladimir ordered his other missile crew to fire on the whaling ship. They had to get loose from the cable and that harpoon gun couldn't be allowed to fire again. Also Poolom Pannarang's men were now in the sail of bridge and had opened fire with automatic weapons.

The harpoon gun was difficult to reload and the whalers retreated under the fire. A missile took out the railing where the gun had been secured and started a fire on board the ship. Jessica and the crew took refuge on the far side of the vessel when the damaged Seawolf helicopter came barreling over and made an controlled crash landing on the vessel!

The landing was as perfect as it could be under the circumstances. The big helicopter came down squarely on the cutting deck for the whale carcasses and remained intact. The crew, marines and Bennett Boyd's team came running out of the helicopter. The crew of the *Yoshino Maru* sprayed down the helicopter with fire hoses, keeping a fire from breaking out.

Jessica Tate and members of the crew of the whaler came running over to the people from the helicopter, helping them and their equipment out of the crippled chopper. She identified herself to Bennett Boyd and the commander of the marines and exclaimed, "We need you to help us with the fire fight with the submarine on the other side of the ship. They're planning to sink this ship!"

Even though dazed by the crash, Bennett Boyd's team and the marines readied their weapons and took up positions along the part of the ship facing the submarine. Their accurate fire changed the tide of the battle. The remaining missile crew was cut down and the fire from Poolom's men contained. Vladimir put the submarine underway and soon the limit of the cable on the *Yoshino Maru* was reached and the strain could not be held—the cable snapped with a loud report and went flying back toward the ship.

Bwana Doc knew he had to act quickly. The commander of the pirate submarine now knew that the *Retter* was nearby and seemed intent on destroying everyone that had seen his boat. He could only guess on why it would want to plunder the old whaling ship, but it clearly wasn't an environmentalist ship, either.

"We need to disable that submarine. I'd rather not kill them if I don't have, too, but it's pretty clear they are planning to sink every ship and the people on them will die in the freezing water. That's not what we came for."

Lavigna had the answer. "Bwana Doc, we can control the detonation of the AM2A3 torpedoes. They are wire guided. We can run them right up the propeller of the submarine and explode

191

them right before impact. With any luck, the propeller will be damaged and the boat will be dead in the water."

"Good! Let's do it," replied Bwana Doc enthusiastically, gratified by the enthusiasm of his hired crew.

The Israeli crew enthusiastically prepped for combat. At last, the real thing—underwater combat!

"Course to target entered, Captain," announced Yuraham who had assumed control of the weapons systems.

"Fire" cried Lavigna, a word he always liked to use.

The DMA23 "Seehecht" torpedo was pushed from the torpedo tube with a blast of compressed air and its electric motors started smoothly in the water, unaffected by the low temperatures. The guidance wire reel began to unwind and the imaging system was working perfectly. Yuraham guided the torpedo perfectly using the ISUS 90-1 Total Control System. Using a ball mouse, he guided the missile straight toward the spinning single massive seven blade propeller in the stern of the Russian built submarine. As it came into view, he abruptly slowed the submarine and let it glide toward the propeller. When it came within a meter or two of the submarine, he detonated the warhead.

The explosion so near the surface was enormous. The stern of the submarine rose completely out of the water. The water boiled as the RDX based explosive in the warhead vaporized and hit the submarine like a boxing glove on a tired fighter's face.

Poolom's face turned ashen as the vessel shook from the shock. He had never experienced anything like this before. He panicked, he hadn't expected anything like this when he had decided to steal the ambergris. "We've got to get out of here. Get an inflatable up on deck, they're going to sink us!"

Vladimir tried to calm him as damage reports came in. "The torpedo didn't actually hit us, it must have blown up before it impacted. We have a few minor leaks, but we're not sinking. We're not getting any sounds from the other ship. She's quiet in the water. No sign she's planning to fire another torpedo."

The panicked pirate Poolom was having none of the Russian's ministrations. "Get us out of range of the fire from the whaling vessel. We're getting off now, I tell you. Get those Zodiacs out. If you don't think they are going to sink us, fine. You can stay with your ship. We're leaving with the ambergris."

Vladimir would do anything to get the pirate and his men off his boat. He ordered his crew to comply. Clearly whoever was firing on him was not intending just to sink the submarine or they already would have done so. He turned the damaged submarine away from the *Yoshino Maru* and headed away from the still firing marines whose bullets were ricocheting harmlessly off the steel hull of the submarine.

Back on the *Yoshino Maru*, things were going well. The fire from the missile had spread a little, but it was being handled by the crew. Luckily injuries were not bad. Several of the Marines had suffered minor injuries from the crash, but everyone had gotten out alive. The threat of the submarine remained. "I don't like it," Captain Sato said, "but we may need to abandon ship. That

193

submarine may still sink us with a torpedo. The catcher ships will be here soon and they will be able to pick us up."

Bennett Boyd agreed they needed to be ready for more trouble. She still had communications with the *Liberty* and the second Seawolf was on the way, armed with torpedoes and missiles this time. The submarine would not get the opportunity to get off a first shot. It was, however, still an hour out and the *Liberty* would be there in three hours. The Japanese destroyer was closer and would be there in two hours. They just had to survive that long.

"Do you think the pirates plan to torpedo us?" Bennett Boyd asked Jessica Tate who clearly knew more about the pirates than anyone else.

"I don't think so. They would have done so already. The question is—where did that explosion come from?"

They looked out on the pirate submarine and saw the Zodiacs being lowered. They braced themselves for another attack by the pirates, but the boats sped off toward the horizon and then, just as unexpectedly, the submarine began to submerge.

The *Harimau* was not in good running order, however. The explosion had damaged the propeller and caused it to make a significant vibration at higher revolutions. She could no longer run silently. Vladimir cursed in Russian. He had to make some headway out of here. He could expect more helicopters or worse, the ship that launched them at any time. But he knew, like all submariners knew, a submarine underwater was always harder to hit than one on the surface. He submerged the vessel almost instinctively as the Zodiacs sped off with Poolom Pannarang and his pirates and headed out away from the *Yoshino Maru* and whatever had torpedoed his submarine.

The people on board the *Yoshino Maru* were still contemplating what to do when a spectacular sight appeared. Like a mechanical Moby Dick, a huge white submarine breached out of the water doing an emergency surface. A beautiful sight, she maneuvered along side the *Yoshino Maru*. A tall man with a large white fur hat and coat emerged on the sail bridge. Putting a megaphone to his mouth, he shouted, "Ahoy, *Yoshino Maru*, Prepare to abandon ship."

Overcoming his astonishment, Captain Sato shouted back, "I require assistance, not to abandon the ship."

"That was not a request. You must abandon ship now. Do not signal for help and I promise that you will not be harmed. If you do not do as I say, you will be sunk," came the reply.

"What's going on?" exclaimed Bennett, stunned by this new development—another submarine out of nowhere. The crew was equally agog.

A large flag broke out over the sail of the submarine; a pirate flag on top of a picture of the earth as seen from outer space. The grinning eyepatched skull leered out at the gaping crewmen of the whaling ship.

"It looks like we've fallen in with another batch of pirates." commented Jessica. "But these may be nicer than the other ones."

D. R. Schneider

The people on the *Yoshino Maru* had no choice but to obey. The life boats were filled first with crewmen and scientists and lowered into the water, leaving behind Captain Sato, Bennett Boyd, Jessica Tate and the navy personnel. They prepared the last lifeboat for launch when they discovered that it had been damaged by gunfire. They informed the *Retter* of their problem.

"Drop your weapons over the side, now" demanded Bwana Doc as crewmembers on the submarine dragged an inflatable boat out of an aft hatch and began filling it with air from a small tank. He could have given them the inflatable and let them go, but he wanted to find out what they knew about the pirate submarine and why it had hijacked the whaling ship.

"What is the name of your vessel, Captain?" called out Bennett Boyd, taking the megaphone from Sato, who could only gape in surprise.

"I'm not the captain, I'm the owner, my name is Bwana Doc and my vessel's name is *Retter der Wale*—the savior of the whales. And who might I have the honor of addressing?"

"I'm Bennett Boyd from Interpol and isn't "your" vessel the "Admiral Mendoza" of the Argentine navy? I believe that man next to you is Captain Lavigna of the Argentine Navy—someone that we would dearly like to talk to."

"*Formerly* of the Argentine Navy on both accounts, madam. Captain Lavigna is now in the employ of Bwana Doc's fleet of ships that do only good," and he bowed his head and doffed his large white fur hat. "We will all be pleased to speak with you once you are on board. Now your weapons, please."

They had little choice. It was clear that the submarine had them outmanned as well as outgunned. He could just torpedo the ship and then pick them up. Bennett Boyd and her team dropped their armament into the sea and with some reluctance the marines followed suit. Jessica dropped her FL90, but palmed her nine millimeter pistol and slipped into the pocket of her pea jacket.

The inflatable motored to the back of the ship to the slipway. In short order they were picked up and brought to the side of the *Retter* where a Jacob's Ladder was lowered. Each member was frisked as they came up and Jessica's gun was easily removed.

"No guns for the passengers. We're pirates that like a peaceable ship, ma'am." grinned Bwana Doc.

Jessica grinned back, unable to resist the charm of the tall man with the ne'er do well air about him. This guy was sexy, thought Jessica.

"Can't blame me for trying. It's me trade," she answered in a mock pirate accent, "And you are Bwana Doc."

"That I am, ma'am, the one the only."

Bennett Boyd was considerably less cheerful. "You're a thief, Bwana Doc. And you're a real pirate. We've heard of you before. You're also wanted for numerous acts of environmental vandalism on a grand scale."

Bwana Doc's face darkened. "Not vandalism, madam. Not vandalism. We'll talk more later, now get below. Blain, keep them

197

under guard. We need to get underwater—more company is on the way."

After the inflatable boat had been recovered and stowed, they made ready to submerge. The fires on the *Yoshino Maru* had subsided, just as Bwana Doc had feared. The flag of Bwana Doc was furled and the sail hatch closed.

Bwana Doc told Captain Lavigna to go ahead. Lavigna gave the order. "Take her down, Mr. Mitzna and take us away from that ship. Ready Torpedoes 2 and 3."

Once a safe distance away at periscope depth, they fired the two torpedoes. One impacted the ship on the side, the other at the slipway that had seen so many dead whales dragged up it. The ship exploded in a mass of flame.

It took her awhile to sink and Bwana Doc recorded each second of it, from impact to the last bit of mast above the water. He had a satisfied look on his face as he looked back at Mr. G, Homeless Pete and Blain, smiled and nodded silently. The environmental pirates had accomplished their task. The whales were safe—at least for awhile.

Chapter 24

Conclusion

"All good things must come to an end"—English proverb

"Helicopter on radar, Captain. I think it's the other Seawolf from the Americans," reported the electronics officer on board the Retter *der Wale*.

"Take us into the thick of ice floes, they'll have a hard time tracking us in the grinding of the ice bergs. The growlers and bergy bits will make a good bit of noise and mask us," ordered Lavigna.

As icebergs melted, they generated continous noise as air trapped by the frozen water was released and bubbled to the surface. The majority of the pieces of ice, known as "growlers" and "bergy bits", were the smallest, but they made the most noise as they melted.

The *Retter der Wale* left the chaotic scene behind. Smoke still poured from some of the surviving Oceanwarriors' ships. The other ships were still dealing with the survivors of the sunken and damaged and caring for their wounded. The Japanese catcher ships were just appearing over the horizon.

The other Seawolf helicopter appeared over the horizon, its crew eager for vengeance. The pilot knew that there was a submarine in the vicinity and began dropping sonobuoys to find it. The Russian's submarine's damaged propellers soon gave it away. The ship began to ping with its active sonar on the submarine, just to let it know he could not get away, whether he liked it or not. The *Liberty* was not far away and the Japanese guided missile destroyer could be seen on the horizon. The Sea Wolf had plenty of fuel; she waited patiently with one of its antisubmarine warfare torpedoes ready to fire if any hostile activity was detected from the submarine.

Back on the *Retter*, Bwana Doc pondered what to do with his rescues. They were really not safe to have around for any length of time. Even unarmed, combat trained men and women were not safe to keep aboard a ship as small as a submarine. It would be best to put them in an inflatable raft and let them make there way back to the *Liberty* or the *Chokai* that was now coming onto the scene. He just didn't want to end up in the sights of either one of these vessels or the Seawolf which he could hear pinging on the pirate submarine. He was deep in the ice floes now and even surfaced his white exterior would make him quite safe from detection as long as there was snow falling. He would just look like another iceberg until anyone was quite close.

Bwana Doc sat down to talk to Bennett Boyd. She had identified herself as an agent of Interpol charged with stopping piracy. She told Bwana Doc, "If I had the power to do it, I would arrest you now. But I know it's pointless to even state it."

Bwana Doc smiled and nodded. "Yes, I don't think the arm of the law is that long, yet. But I want you to understand why I do what I do. You don't have to like it. You have a job to do, I know.

I respect that. I do what I do because your way of doing things, the orderly, civilized way, doesn't work."

"What do you mean, it doesn't work? Everyone is an environmentalist now. It's the most popular thing there is."

"Does that make any difference? Has it made any difference? The world is still being destroyed by people. Has anything been done about whaling in the Antarctic after the decades of protests and activism? They were still killing whales, until today. Those Oceanwarriors people, God rest their souls, were as ineffectual as a petition in stopping whaling. They had been trying for years. After today, the Japanese won't kill whales in the Antarctic anymore. No new factory ships will be built because it never was economic to do whaling anyway. It was simple Japanese nationalism that fueled the *Yoshino Maru*, not a need for whale meat protein."

"But you can't just break the law," replied Boyd. "Laws are for all people."

"Where was the law for the whales, for the sharks, for every other living thing that gets in the way of what mankind wants. I'll tell you where. It was nowhere." answered Bwana Doc angrily.

"What do you plan to do with us? Are we someone that needs to be gotten rid of too?"

"I don't kill people except in self defense. Life is sacred to us, unlike so many "environmentalists". Shortly, we're going to move to the edge of the ice pack and let you go in the inflatable. The snow is building up. We'll give you a radio and we'll also send a message to the *Chokai* and the *Liberty* and the catcher ships. We'll also stay around until you're picked up. I don't think you will be able to find us in this icepack. You've got to take care of that pirate submarine anyway. That's your real problem, not me."

"You know I have to come after you now. Before, you just operated in the shadows. We had heard of you, but this is too big of an incident. I'm a pirate hunter, that's what I do."

"I can't think a more beautiful pursuer. I look forward to it. Catch me if you can," said Bwana Doc with a wide grin and a twinkle of his ocean blue eyes.

He then went to visit Jessica. He expected her to be much less communicative since he still thought of her as one of the pirates. When she turned out to be an ex-navy Seal working Naval Intelligence, he was surprised how open she was about her info. She didn't really care about the whalers at all. She was concerned about pirates, and while Bwana Doc might be some kind of strange enviro-pirate, he clearly wasn't a pirate like the evil Poolom Pannarang. And she was very attracted to him. She revealed the story of the ambergris and where Poolom had gotten his submarine. Bwana Doc's face showed his dismay.

"They would intentionally want to kill sick whales so that they could get ambergris to make a new, special perfume. That's much worse than killing them for meat."

"I agree. And Poolom would have killed all the crew and as many other witnesses as he could find. You saved a lot of good people today."

202

Bwana Doc nodded his head. "You saved a lot of good people yourself. The Japanese whalers aren't bad people. They are doing a job. I believe in the sanctity of all life. I wouldn't have killed Poolom Pannarang either. I would have turned him over to you and your people."

"But you don't believe in the law either. You stole this submarine."

"Well, yes," said Bwana Doc with a smile. "I believe the ends do justify the means as long as the means have limits. The Argentines didn't really need this submarine. Most countries don't need the armed forces they have. They are a burden on the country that should be eased so that more money would be available to help their poor and their environment. I'm putting this submarine to a much better use. Now every year there will be a thousand more whales in the ocean. That's a good thing. There is a lot more things that need to be cleaned up and this submarine may be helpful to do that. We'll be keeping it."

"How are you going to hide a submarine?" Jessica was astonished by the boldness of his actions.

"That's for me to know and you to find out," Bwana Doc replied impishly, "It's still a big planet and I've been blessed with a lot of resources to help save it. I think we'll get away with it. We've done a few things already, but I think it's time to expand the scope of our activities. For all the talk about it, and all the supposed action, the environment is in a crisis stage now. After all, we're helped by the fact that really no one cares as much as we do about the problems we want to fix. Each industry or government just looks at their own activities. There's little global policing of the abuses going on."

"I hear you're letting us go soon," replied Jessica, still taking in the magnitude of his vision and his ambitions for the future. This was a man to be reckoned with.

"That's right. We'll be putting you in an inflatable and letting the U.S. and Japanese navy know where you are. You'll be fine."

"You know we'll be using what we know to try to find you. You won't ever be safe."

"None of us are ever safe, Miss Tate. None of us. Safety is an illusion."

"Call me Jessica. I like you and what you are doing. I have an employer who, I am sure is not going to like at all what you are doing, but I do."

"I'm glad to hear that. I hope you don't have to get involved in any more dangerous undercover jobs like you had."

"You never know in my line of work. But I'd like to stay in touch with you. Use this email address," she said, scribbling on a piece of paper and handing it to him. "It's discrete and untraceable on both ends."

"Thank you," he said. "I don't believe I've ever run into anyone quite like you before."

"And I know I haven't run into anyone like you, Bwana Doc." she replied softly, looking him straight in the eye.

The marines, Interpol people, and Jessica Tate were put back into the submersible. Through the growing snowstorm, they could vaguely see the shapes of the *Liberty* and *Chokai* in the distance along with some of the catcher ships.

Yuruham gave them a heading to take. "Just dodge the ice floes," he said, "we're submerging now and sending a message to the *Liberty*. You should be fine, but we'll hang around and make sure."

The inflatable sped off into the snowstorm, Bennett Boyd already talking into the radio.

"Take us down to periscope depth and keep an eye on them, Captain. There's one person in that boat I particularly want to get back home," said Bwana Doc.

"Will do, Bwana Doc. Let's get below. Dive the boat when ready, Mr. Mitzna," Lavigna ordered.

The *Retter* sank beneath the waves. The water was alive with the sound of the ice, thawing, jostling against itself. They sent the signal and waited. Soon they saw one of the catcher boats headed toward the dinghy. The submarine cut her engines and dropped down into deep water and became as silent as a tomb. They drifted with the noisy ice above; one with the ocean, listening for any effort to find them.

Meanwhile, the pirate submarine remained submerged and trying to get away, but the sound of the screws of the *Liberty* and *Chokai* sealed their fate as far as Vladimir was concerned. The U.S. ship would probably not sink them, but the Japanese would have no compunction once the *Yoshino Maru's* crew was back. He gave the order to surface.

The grey submarine came up to an Antarctic summer seascape of ice flows and a few blowing snowflakes in the air. Vladimir took up a bed sheet from one of the crew's bunks and told one of them to attach it to the sail. Flapping in the wind, the flag of surrender looked forlorn, like a misplaced iceberg. He sent a radio signal to the Seawolf above telling them he was surrendering.

The surfacing of the *Harimau* was the perfect distraction Bwana Doc needed to silently slip away from the confused scene. Bennett's urgent signaling about another submarine was too confusing for Hayford—he had a submarine in sight and nothing else on sonar. The *Liberty* headed toward the submarine. Faster than the Chokai, he was alongside within minutes. Hayford was fascinated. He'd never seen a Russian built diesel electric submarine up this close and certainly never seen a pirate submarine. He ordered his crew to be ready to receive prisoners and ordered boats sent over to pick them. "Rig for a tow as well. I don't think that boat can go too far under its own power. She looks pretty banged up. I'll need to ask command about how we handle this. We don't have a yardarm to hang 'em or a plank for them to walk.'

"Ms. Boyd, her team, the captain of the *Yoshino Maru* and the marines have been heard from, Captain. They are O.K. They also have someone who they say was with the pirates but isn't one of them, it's the Naval Intelligence operative. One of the catcher boats is picking them up. And Ms. Boyd keeps going on about a big white submarine." said the communications officer.

"Well, one thing at a time—we've got one submarine to take care of now," Hayford replied, "That will have to wait. Get them aboard as soon as is convenient. Get a squad of marines up here to take charge of these pirate submariners."

Back in the Antarctic, Captain Rolway of the "Green Star", one of the Oceanwarriors ships that had not been damaged, was surprised to see two zodiacs speeding toward him. Too far away to see their launching from the submarine, he surmised incorrectly that these might be survivors from either from the *Yoshino Maru* or the submarine that attacked him. As they came alongside, a grinning tall man with dark skin and hair stood up in the zodiac, a large bright yellow box beside him.

"Permission to come aboard, Captain," he said in a happy voice. "We've had a rough day as have you."

"If you're from that submarine or the Japanese whaler, you'll have to wait, the Navy wants to speak with you."

"It wasn't exactly a request, Captain," as the other pirates in the Zodiac revealed their collection of submachine guns.

Poolom Pannarang had found a ride home to Indonesia.

The *Retter der Wale* slipped quietly away from the scene on minimum power. Once well away, they made course for Hobart, Tasmania to rendezvous with the *Alistair Billings*. Hayford and Bennett Boyd initiated a search for the second submarine, but she was far out of detection range. The *Billings* was already back at sea by the time they found that she was in port at Hobart. Bwana Doc moored the *Retter der Wale* in the moon pool of the ship and then took both ships to an out-of-the way port on the east coast of Africa to wait for the next time they might be needed on a mission. From there, the team made their way back to their homes, ready to await Bwana Doc's call for another mission.

Epilogue

At the meeting of the International Whaling Commission, Japan demanded to know the identity of the party that sank its whaling ship. No one could identify or locate an individual named Bwana Doc. An unsigned letter is read that informs the members that any country conducting whaling will find that its ships will encounter "extremely expensive technical difficulties". Following the meeting, Iceland and Norway discretely announce that their shore whaling fleets will spend the future season in port due to "economic factors". After consultations the Japanese did likewise. Whaling by industrial nations was over. Subsistence fishermen like the Innuit would catch a few whales, but these would be fewer than one hundred per year for the entire world.

Bennett Boyd assigned several members of her team to finding Bwana Doc, without success. Jessica Tate resigned from the Navy and her whereabouts are presently equally unknown.

The pirates captured on the submarine were tried in Japanese courts for piracy and sentenced to long terms. Poolom Pannarang made it safely back to Indonesia—several members of the *Green Star*'s crew joined his pirates. The rest of the Oceanwarriors were set free by the pirate after being robbed, of course. Most of them left the Oceanwarriors organization afterwards. With no whaling ships to chase, Roane Sander went on an international speaking tour and wrote a book about his thrilling adventure with the pirates and how he had managed to sink the Japanese whaling fleet despite all the efforts of the Japanese navy to stop him.

The fresh ambergris? With no space to refrigerate it on the *Green Star*, it aged too much and the addictive chemical was lost. Poolom did sell it to Gamali who in turn sold it to Vaneel. His research people found it worthless. Chevillac's people on the other hand were eventually able to synthesize and patent the chemical and produced a new perfume named appropriately "Addictive". It was eventually banned by several governments, but not before making Chevillac a large amount of money. Poolom used the money from the sale of the useless ambergris to finance a new pirate fleet, but without a submarine this time.

Bwana Doc and his Austin collaborators settled back into their discrete lives, but not until they had a celebration that lasted for days. With plenty of Monopolowa vodka and Hendrick's gin, of course.

NEXT: Bwana Doc Stops the Shark Finners!

Saving the Whales

D. R. Schneider

www.ingramcontent.com/pod-product-compliance
Lightning Source LLC
Chambersburg PA
CBHW050930120626
46552CB00001B/130